THE STILL STORM

'A superb tale... disturbingly erotic... exquisite characterisation... *Tristesse* Saga...

Françoise Sagan achieved international acclaim with her first novel, Bonjour Tristesse, *published in 1954 when she was only nineteen. She has written many novels, some of which have become films, and several plays. W. H. Allen published her previous novel,* The Painted Lady, *which was greeted with great enthusiasm by critics in France, Britain and America.*

Also by Françoise Sagan and published by Star

THE PAINTED LADY

THE STILL STORM

Françoise Sagan

Translated from the French by
Christine Donougher

A STAR BOOK
published by
the Paperback Division of
W. H. ALLEN & Co. PLC

A Star Book
Published in 1985
by the Paperback Division of
W. H. Allen & Co. PLC
44 Hill Street, London W1X 8LB

First published in France by
Jean-Jacques Pauvert *chez* Julliard, 1983,
under the title *Un Orage Immobile*
First published in Great Britain
by W. H. Allen, 1984

Printed and bound in Great Britain by
Anchor Brendon Ltd, Tiptree, Essex

ISBN 0 352 31611 X

To Peggy Roche

IF ONE DAY SOMEONE ELSE should read these pages – if an author's blind vanity or some quirk of fate prevent me from destroying them – that reader should know that it is for my own recollection, and not for the entertainment of others, that I embark on this account of the summer of 1832 and the years that followed. Above all, the reader should know that for those who played a part in these events – the torturers, the victims, or, like myself, the helpless witnesses – I wish only one thing: that they should forget. I wish that they should suppress the memory as relentlessly as the leaden skies oppressed us that first summer in this normally gentle province of Aquitaine.

I am old now, beyond loving or being loved. No one believes me when I claim, as so many men of my age do, that I am reconciled to this state of affairs. Well, it is wrong to disbelieve me. In a few years' time, when my earthly remains are buried beneath the cypress trees in the little cemetery at Nersac, if, as well as some kind soul to mourn my passing, there is anyone present malicious enough to derive some pleasure from my death, his satisfaction will be ill-founded. It is the funeral of a man long since dead that he will be attending. I died thirty years ago. I have endured the past thirty years as a mere survivor of those searing summers.

In 1832 I was thirty years old, a young man older than my years, but still naive. As a bachelor who had inherited one of the best legal practices in the province, I was a highly eligible match and a fine figure of a man for those who prized health above elegance. The hair grew low on my high forehead. I had the eyes of a faithful gun-dog (how I wished them more assertive), my mouth was strong and my chin receded slightly. I had broad shoulders, and a ruddy complexion which attested to the vigour of my sturdy frame. The only features of which I was proud were my hands, whose long slender fingers drew admiring comments from women.

Women . . . I had known few intimately, even after several visits to Paris as a student. I had suffered a protracted and ridiculous passion for a provincial temptress already then past her prime; undertaken two or three liaisons with dissatisfied married women; and bestowed no more than condescending glances on the young girls who were meant, soon, to provide me with a choice of wife. The only woman I ever really loved was Elisa, my mother's maid, but after a year of tentative lovemaking, despite all my entreaties, Elisa had run away from me and a scandal that might never have been. Elisa, and she alone, loved me somewhat, and thawed me a little in matters of the heart. But only a very little. All my experience in this area of life had caused me nothing but distress or frustration – a fate I thought common to all bachelors of my age and of my class living in the provinces at that time.

In 1832, Angoulême quite properly had its own set, presided over with great gusto, as indeed was fitting, by the prefect's wife. Madame Artemise d'Aubec was the very same who had in the past inflamed my passions and not deigned to extinguish them for eighteen long months. It now seemed to me that this seductress was too tall, too thin, her hair too blonde, her voice too shrill – and she was too old. I am still occasionally dismayed to have once thought her so attractive, though it must be said in my defence that I was twenty at the time of my original infatuation, of which I feel embarrassed to this day. And, I might add, others suffered the rigours of her virtue less than I. Artemise d'Aubec ruled both her husband and her suitors with the same show of tyranny that her personal fortune allowed her. It was rumoured that her father had taken advantage of fleeing emigrés – and of his position – to amass this wealth, but the fact of the matter is that, throughout the ten years of her reign, there was an endless succession of balls, poetry recitals, picnics, superb dinners, and so on. Not to be invited to one of her balls was a disgrace; not to accept an invitation was the utmost effrontery. Knowing this, she would neglect to invite a number of people, while one or two of those asked would contrive to forget the date of a party; and for a whole season it would be the talk of the town.

It might seem strange that I should speak so harshly of a woman with whom I was, after all, in love for eighteen months, but she deserves no less. A woman's affairs with other men might cool the ardour of a very young man. But to stop loving a woman because of what she is and what she has done to him, a man must be very disillusioned. He has to be so robbed of his illusions that he might die of the sadness and the shame of it.

BUT I AM DIGRESSING. WE are in Angoulême in the spring of 1832 and, despite a few disturbances, Louis-Philippe rules over France. The rich are rich, the poor are poor, as always, and the bourgeoisie are content – and they are the only political barometer in this country. All is well throughout Aquitaine . . . It is important to know what Aquitaine is like to appreciate fully my account of what happened. And I realise that I cannot help addressing myself to an ideal reader, one who is prepared to be entertained, is ready to believe my story and to be moved by it. I risk exposing myself to ridicule, but what does that matter? I have nothing else to do of any importance. I am hypnotised by my hand – it is still well formed, but now marred by knotted veins – as it moves across this thick, white, almost floury paper adding one little blue mark to another. The ink is the bluest of blues and the inkpot whiter than white.

This intensity I have never experienced in the execution of any of my legal duties. There must be something special involved, as if writers were miraculously endowed with a childlike innocence when they write . . . Only a child would become so engrossed in such pointless symbols and devote so much energy to so futile a task. The futility of my own endeavour is all too clear to me.

My window is on the top floor of my house. (The peasants call it my 'château', the gentry refer to it as my 'establishment', while the burghers of Angoulême, ever down-to-earth, call it my 'residence'.) And the view from my window is of typical Charente countryside: a low-lying hill looks as though it is sinking into a verdant plain, where golden fields are bordered by poplars and traversed by a slow-moving river. Over the plain the sky extends as far as the eye can see. Despite the little, round, prancing clouds – pink, white, blue, and bright red in the west at sunset – the sky dominates the landscape. It seems to rest on our meadows, our churches, our little towns, lying heavily on our land and stretching to the horizon on all sides, day after day, and not a single ear of corn or blade of grass escapes its overbearing presence. The weather is of more importance here than elsewhere because the sky is closer and the sunshine more direct. The nights are darker, the winds wilder, and the heat and the snow more still. The houses in this area are big without being massive, generally attractive, white or grey, with a style of portal which distinguishes them from the square, squat houses in the Beauce, or the pinker, taller, and more narrow houses in the Midi. This is a part of the country marked by restraint, where the people have their dignity, are friendly without being familiar, honest but not ruthlessly so, cheerful but in moderation. In short, it is a place where people take some pride in their neighbours.

This is by way of explaining that the woman who arrived in our midst in 1832 – in fact it would be truer to say she returned to us then – and in whom we, the citizens of Angoulême and inhabitants of Saintonge, could take great pride, was not a Parisian exile nor an eccentric foreigner, but one of our own. She had been brought up in accordance with our customs, our manners and our ways. She was French, of course, but, far more important, she was a child of this province. Her name was Flora de Margelasse, and her family were minor but long-established aristocrats from Jarnac. Their château (even the gentry referred to it as such) had been virtually abandoned for nearly forty years. In the course of those forty years, the de Margelasse family, who were among the last to flee, learned that aristocrats were no longer being beheaded in France. This they told to their only daughter, born in exile in 1805, who later married an Englishman, and then was widowed. Her parents, saddened by her grief, decided to bring her home to France. They disposed of their property in England, but both died before leaving the country. Flora made her way to France alone. By the time she arrived at Jarnac, the family had been completely forgotten and no one had ever heard of Flora de Margelasse.

She arrived in the spring, having spent two years in Paris, where she learned to speak the language of her birth to perfection, a perfection emphasised by a very slight English accent. She also became acquainted with the most seductive and most dangerous part of France – the capital city. And it worked like a tonic on her. For had she stayed in England, Flora might have remained a widow. However, in Paris, she rapidly became a young woman who was destined to remarry. For two years she refused even to countenance the idea, apparently turning down the opportunity to abandon her widowhood on many occasions. But Flora was never meant to be a widow. Some women are born

13

widows, just as others are born mothers, and others are natural spinsters, or wives, or mistresses. And it was to these last two categories that Flora de Margelasse obviously belonged. She was born to share her life with a man, but a man who could laugh with her as well as protect her. This was exactly what Lord Desmond Knight, her first husband, had been able to offer her during their five years of marriage, and she had accepted and reciprocated without reserve a love that was mutual, trusting, and passionate, in which their bodies, their hearts and their minds seemed in perfect harmony with one another. On that fateful day when Desmond Knight's horse returned to the stables without its rider, just like an episode in romantic fiction, Flora was twenty-four. She was twenty-six when she arrived in Angoulême. By the end of the summer of 1835, she had turned thirty, on 23 September to be precise, but that was no longer of any importance – not even to her. Even I attached no weight to that date, despite the fact that I was the notary, the man of law whose most crucial role in effect is to testify to the significance of dates, to ratify with the seal of law the legitimate possession of earthly goods, to pronounce cast-iron judgements on the rights and responsibilities of individuals. And yet at the end of that summer of 1835 I felt that what I was inscribing in my law books would not survive me, or my great-nephews, or the grandchildren of my clerks. I felt as if I were just scribbling, that what I wrote was shallow and meaningless, completely devoid of interest. And while my personal distress was in no way connected with my clients, it robbed me of any confidence in my assurances to them, and destroyed my faith in any guarantees, legal or otherwise, that I might give them. The only thing I could promise them was the terrible taste of ashes which now fills my mouth from morning to night. I hope I am not the only one to experience it. I hope no one is spared this. Sleep, sorrowful, happy Sleep, you alone have I loved, desired, longed for, whole nights on end, as perhaps I have never loved nor desired any woman. Except Flora, of course. For I know of no man worthy of the name who would not have done everything possible to secure Flora's happiness. And similarly, no man would have failed to try at all costs to restore her happiness, even at his own expense, when she had ceased to be happy.

So, on 10 April 1832, before anyone had seen her or passed her carriage in the streets of Jarnac, Flora de Margelasse sent to me and to many others an invitation stamped with a seal that seemed vaguely familiar to me. The de Margelasse crest was a lion rampant on a field of wheat beneath an unsettled sky, and bore the obscure legend *Virtus sive malus*. I must have chanced upon this crest in my legal files, and suddenly I could see in my mind's eye, against the background of a blazing fire, a berlin coach speeding away from the de Margelasse domain, only twelve miles from my study. But after all, I was only thirty, and I must have seen this stirring image of the French Revolution in my god-daughter's school history-books. Anyway, by means of this card, Lady Desmond Knight, widow of Lord Desmond Knight, informed me that her household was re-established at Margelasse and conveyed the pleasure it would give her to welcome me there, 'and all the friends with whom she had neither had the occasion nor the good fortune to acquaint herself sooner'. In her invitation she referred to her father and mother, Odon and Blanche de Margelasse, who had died in Norfolk two years previously, and who would share her delight – had I believed in an after-life – in my presence under their roof.

Flora's parents were cousins. They had grown up together and eventually married; their blood kinship, it seems, had never presented the slightest obstacle to their union. But Flora was born a long time afterwards, after ten unsuccessful attempts to have a child had undermined her mother's health. She remained fragile until her death. When she died, Flora's father was heartbroken and he too died shortly after. This double bereavement, following very soon after the loss of her husband, had prompted Flora to leave England. She returned to a France with which she was unfamiliar and a province of which she knew nothing, beyond the fact that some farm-workers, loyal and faithful to an almost fanatical degree, had maintained her father's estate. It was then that Angoulême and its environs, and all levels of its society, suddenly learned of the existence of a young lady of Margelasse to whom the estate belonged, and learned too that this young lady was a wealthy widow who was returning from England to settle amongst us. I make no mention of what else some people believed they knew, which was as improbable, fanciful and bizarre as the products of provincial imagination can be at the end of a tediously cold and frosty winter. As for myself, since my grandfather had been the notary for Margelasse in the past, I was politely requested on another card if I could possibly come and see Flora the following week.

On Tuesday, 15 April 1832, I presented myself at the château. I have my diary for that year in front of me, open at that page, across which I have written with all the confidence of a young man: 'Three o'clock Marge-lasse', without any punctuation, just like that – 'Three o'clock Margelasse'. Alas, destiny does not always employ her heralds to announce what twists of fate she has in store, or else her heralds have tired of winking knowingly at us poor mortals, undiscerning as we are! And that day I greatly enjoyed the ride to Margelasse on my handsome chestnut stallion. The weather was fine and the woods on the way were filled with the scent of lily-of-the-valley, and the fields smelled of young grass. The old round château looked enchanting in the spring light, with its poplars and meadows where two black-and-white horses frisked about. Those two fine animals caught my eye and I lingered on the terrace to watch them.

Flora de Margelasse came out of the house and approached me with her hand outstretched. Embarrassed, I took her hand and bowed, already aware that this woman was kind-hearted and beautiful. When at last I was able to look at her as openly as she looked at me, those long almond-shaped eyes seemed already familiar to me, as did her girlish complexion, fine features, and her firm mouth that was smiling and tender; I recognised the gracefulness of her neck and her hands, her radiant refined blondeness, the sparkle of her eyes, her alto voice, her gaiety. All this I recognised, and I wanted to marry her there and then, to give her children, to cherish her, to protect her for the rest of my life.

Though old in my ways, I was still a naive young man, and in the past I had stupidly loved a heartless woman. But it was ten years since then, and while I was not cold, neither was I a passionate man readily inclined to fall in love. My heart was much slower to commit itself than my body, and my mind much slower than my heart. The reader will therefore understand how smitten I was when I almost said to Flora de Margelasse 'Marry me' instead of 'My compliments'. A faint-hearted man had good reason to feel bewildered; even a man more bold than I might have been taken aback.

IT IS THREE WEEKS SINCE I last opened this notebook. Writing and remembering, both, have dangerous and painful consequences. The other day as I finished describing our meeting, it seemed to me the blue ink-marks on my white notepaper faded and disappeared. I imagined that these sheets of wove paper had flown away – the pages of my diary, my love-letters and the autumn leaves had all been whisked away while I stood trembling once more on that terrace.

I could smell the grass in the meadow, the more subtle perfume of Flora's hand, and behind me I thought I heard the sound of the bit in my horse's mouth as it tossed its head. I saw Flora's beautiful blue eyes that were gay and tender. I saw my youth and hers. I remembered that mad impulse to say to her: 'Will you marry me?', and a ridiculous but heartfelt sadness, a silly but genuine regret that I did not ask her suddenly made unbearable a memory of sunshine and shadow and scent. I was so upset by this that I almost abandoned my account altogether. And yet here I am again, unable not to write, despite my disgust at my own unhappiness, despite my hatred of complacency, of forced nostalgia, of the past and lost happiness. I continue to write for no reason and for no one's benefit. The scratching of this pen is an end in itself, though this paper seems ever more white, ever more resistant to my increasingly illegible scribbling. The intimacy of these pages is hateful to me, isolated as I am in this house (or residence, château, pile of bricks and mortar – call it what you will) that no one ever visits any more.

The only people who come here now are my placid short-sighted housekeeper, her helpers, her placid long-sighted husband, and the priest at Nersac who cannot accept my loss of faith, or at least the fact that I told him of it in a moment of unpardonable ill-humour. With the exception of these uninspiring but well-meaning and harmless souls, for whom the future takes the form of death and promises nothing, no one has been here since Flora's final visit. I remember her as I saw her then. She wore a dress of crumpled silk, and her superb profusion of blonde hair danced in the bright sunlight like an oriflamme captured from the enemy that was brandished in derision over her face now white and ageless and sexless.

THERE IS NO DOUBT I was the first man in Angoulême to fall in love with Flora de Margelasse, but there is no distinction in that since I was the first to set eyes on her. However, I was certainly not her only admirer, and I believe that by the end of the ball, the first ball held at Margelasse, I had a considerable number of rivals. No credit is due to them either, since Flora was charm itself. That evening provided the first but most conclusive evidence of this. For Flora was inclined to be mysterious – a trait I deplore but which is, after all, the essence of a woman's flirtatiousness – and she had contrived not to be properly seen by anyone before that evening.

Until then she had left Margelasse only to ride out in a horse and trap. She drove herself – a custom brought with her from England which scandalised the ladies of Angoulême – with spirit and at great speed. The immediate instinct of the few men she happened to ride past during her first days here was to stand aside and protect themselves; there was no thought of sharing their fragile existence with this amazon. The black-and-

23

white horses were two fine English cobs imported from across the Channel, and she drove them like the wind, with a firm hand. As she flashed past, bystanders merely glimpsed her hair flying out behind her, her eyes shining with excitement, and a boyish silhouette.

The good ladies whose husbands worked in the prefect's office, and who were used to modestly gathering their skirts to step in and out of their carriages, found her sporting attitude quite shameless. They even whispered amongst themselves that Flora de Margelasse must have handled her husband in the same way – with a whip (although she had never yet been seen to use one on her horses) – and this was how she had driven him to his grave, galloping about without a parasol. The wife of the prefect, in whose presence I was foolish enough to admit that Madame Knight née de Margelasse was not without a certain appeal, and in whose presence I was inconceivably stupid enough to blush as I spoke, was bristling with anticipation well in advance of the ball, an occasion which was likely to call into question her position of absolute authority.

The few servants and cooks kindly sent over to help the unfortunate newcomer to settle in had subsequently shrouded themselves in disconcerting silence. It seemed this woman was able to win their affection from the moment they met her – which upset a good number of plans and frustrated the curiosity of many.

The only man to have seen her and spoken to her was myself, the well-known buffoon Nicholas Lomont, whose position as notary had won him that privilege. I was beseiged with questions, as if I had spent the past fortnight at the feet of Flora de Margelasse. In fact I had seen her only three times, for half an hour on each occasion, when we discussed business. She wanted me

24

to advise her on her affairs, comitting to my charge all matters relating to her property and her estate with a disarming spontaneity and trustfulness.

I should have welcomed her confidence had I not realised that the sense of security Flora de Margelasse enjoyed in my company was the most ominous sign that she would never love me. I was not so stupid as to be unaware that there is no love where there is no fear of love, and Flora was not afraid of me. She had no reason to be afraid, but by the same token, because I was already deeply in love with her, I had every reason to be frightened.

I will not go into further detail as to how and why I had instantly fallen in love with Flora de Margelasse and would love her until the day I died. This account of the bare facts will amply convey that. Let us simply say that right from the start I was resigned to loving Flora; worse, I was proud to love her, proud in advance of all that she would bring upon me, including the cruellest unhappiness. Whatever happened, nothing in any way connected with her would make me lose heart. That was all I knew, and this I had understood from the moment I first set eyes on her.

THE BALL, THEN, WAS ATTENDED by the whole of Angoulême, a large group from Cognac, numerous nobles from all parts of the country, a few men of letters from Paris – to the general astonishment of the local guests, as if Paris were peopled by nothing but degenerates and street-walkers – and it was even graced by the supremely exotic presence of one or two English couples. To be more precise in my description, I should say that from the very beginning of the ball I felt like a traitor, without knowing whom I was betraying, nor why. It is a feeling I had rarely experienced and nothing in my life seemed to warrant it.

Artemise d'Aubec was there, with her husband, Honoré-Anthelme d'Aubec. As I mentioned earlier, he was prefect of Angoulême, and expected to move on to the post in Lyons and eventually reach the capital, the prize to which, no matter what people may say, every provincial bureaucrat in France aspires. The political and material ambitions of Honoré d'Aubec were common knowledge. There was an unspoken agreement between the d'Aubecs, the French Government, and the town of Angoulême that, at the end of his career, this ruddy-faced bear of a man, Honoré d'Aubec, would be an influential millionaire, and his wife would hold all Paris in thrall with the power of her shrill voice.

Meanwhile, Flora's arrival was a potential threat to Artemise's supremacy, and I was not the only one who realised that Flora would have to make some sign of allegiance to the prefect's wife. Unless she took her place among the ranks of Artemise's ladies-in-waiting, Flora would have to resign herself to solitude in her château, and might even be obliged to leave Angoulême if her disdain were too evident. And I did not doubt for an instant that this disdain would manifest itself, and would simply be the contempt of a noble spirit for a lesser one, of a person without affectation for a poseur, of a charming woman for one who believed herself so. Frankly, I anticipated the worst at this ball. While I was apprehensive, I half relished the confrontation, still being young enough to imagine myself offering my arm – prepared to sacrifice my reputation and honour – to a woman beset by vipers. I pictured myself melodramatically striking poor Honoré, or capping Artemise's snubs with outrageous insolence – I, the man who never has a ready answer when needed, but stumbles upon one three days later. When Madame d'Aubec's carriage drew up at the steps to Madame Knight's château, I thought two worlds were about to collide. Yet what I saw – as did everyone present – was a meeting of two women who had the good manners and breeding to behave as if they were the closest and most affectionate of friends.

So this first ball was a success. And as it was Artemise d'Aubec herself who made the pronouncement, it was generally agreed, once and for all, that Lady Flora Knight née de Margelasse was a delightful woman. The good ladies of Angoulême would regard it their pleasure and duty to lighten the burden of her widowhood. And no doubt one day there might be among the higher echelons of Angoulême society a man of sufficient charm to provide the ultimate consolation; they would make a splendid couple, and certainly reflect no discredit – quite the contrary – on this little Versailles of the Charente that our fine old town had become. When she left the ballroom at Margelasse at dawn, Artemise d'Aubec already had plans for a second marriage. And one could detect that air of suppressed joy with which the thought of another's happiness always endowed her (while the thought of that same person's unhappiness conferred on her an altogether more exuberant joy). Anyway, she embraced her dear Flora a dozen times, while Flora suffered herself to be embraced. And in the light of the evidence I had to acknowledge that my grandmother, my aunts, Elisa and Artemise were right – I was just a stupid young man who possessed the social graces of a provincial rustic.

THE PICNICS BEGAN, AND THE dinners, the parties, the promenades beneath the trees in town continued as before, the only difference being that Flora now attended them, and I was completely and hopelessly in love with her. And so the years 1832 and 1833 passed like a dream, although they should have seemed like decades, and lasted for ever. Yet I was certain of nothing but my own love. For you can never be sure of a woman's indifference. You begin to believe she means no, and a glance makes you think she means yes. You get up in despair, and a touch of the hand sends you to bed delirious with hope.

I should have remained in that state: those endless ups and downs would eventually have left me in a limbo of peacefulness, half-way between sadness and joy, no longer dependent on her nor on my feelings for her, but once more a rational man. However, I was young and reckless. I wanted to be told what I already knew. And, must I admit it? I felt resentful towards Flora because of my own silence. After two weeks, she could not be unaware of my feelings; but she never gave the slightest hint of it. There are not many courses open to a woman who is loved but does not return your love. There is escape in silence, a cruel silence of which I knew Flora to be incapable, but I saw that she had no choice. I thought that Flora, in order to maintain our calm and – for her – easy-going friendship, had chosen to ignore what was rending my heart in two. So one stormy evening I asked if I could see her alone. She agreed at once, without even asking the reason, or betraying the least curiosity.

I was trembling when I arrived at Margelasse the following evening before dinner. I was trembling in anticipation of the wound she must inflict on me, and I was trembling because of the happy fool, the mad child in me who had woken me two or three times during the night to ask: 'Suppose she was to fall into your arms . . . ? What if it has all been a terrible misunderstanding . . . ? And if she has been waiting, brokenhearted as you are, for a single word . . . ?' Once the lamp was relit and I was restored to my senses, I would willingly have smothered this mad child under a pillow, but no man is capable of destroying the childish hopes that sustain him.

Flora was waiting for me outside near the greenhouse, which she was considering with the scant interest that marked her attitude towards inanimate objects in general. She liked only what moved – people, dogs, horses, the wind. She was wearing a dress of light grey cloth – of exactly what fabric I do not know – that rustled when she walked and caught the setting sun whichever way she turned, so that she looked as if she were dressed in pink as well as grey.

'Would you like to go inside,' she said, 'or would you rather sit here?'

Without waiting for a reply, she lowered herself into a cane garden seat that graced the terrace, no doubt expecting me to sit next to her; but I sat opposite in a comfortable armchair. I looked up at her with what I hoped was a serious expression; it must have been a fixed look of bewilderment.

'I wanted to tell you . . .' I began.

She was studiously examining her hands that were pressed close together, but I hesitated so long she finally raised her eyes.

'Flora . . .' I finally beseeched her.

'If only I could . . .' she said.

And as our eyes met, we saw we were both in the same depths of despair. She stood up, or I rose first, I no longer remember, and it was she who comforted me, who took me in her arms – although I was a good head taller – and she rocked me gently while I clung to her shoulder, heaving and sobbing uncontrollably. I had not wept since the death of my father fifteen years previously.

We exchanged a few embarrassed words, and both apologised before sitting down together on the same garden seat. Flora's phrase had said it all – 'If only I could . . .' – and mine that followed – 'It doesn't matter.' And it had thereby been acknowledged that I would love her as long as I lived, and that she would never be mine.

One evening a few weeks later, having drunk too much, I pleaded with her, as if begging for alms, to let me share her bed for just a couple of hours. Her pride as a woman was offended – not pride in her virtue but in her sensuality. She said she hoped that after two hours I should not be sated but, on the contrary, that my desire for her should be even greater. She had always taken seriously those matters some said were of no importance, and nothing would move her to try and

33

simplify them, nor indeed degrade them – not even pity.

A little later, when we were more composed, I muttered some reproach against her silence and her pretence of being unaware of my passion. But when I mentioned the words 'silence of convenience', she was indignant.

'It might have occurred to you,' she said, speaking to me curtly for the first time, 'that it was for your sake I said nothing, and not my own. There are men for whom it is ten times worse once things have actually been said. You might have been like that yourself. By not saying anything, you might have hoped to give your feelings a chance to fade away. There would have been nothing silly about that, I assure you. Words are often more harmful than deeds.'

'So it was wrong of me to speak?' I said, but she smiled and covered my hand with hers to stop me.

'No,' she replied, 'since that was what you wanted to do.'

FOR TWO YEARS LIFE WAS a waking dream – at least it was for me – and I am ashamed to admit, once more, that they were two happy years. I saw Flora nearly every day. There was no one Flora loved more than me. She went away only a few times during the winter of 1833–4, spending a week on each occasion in Paris, with friends of her husband. She went to the theatre, to concerts, to poetry recitals. I alone knew she also spent time with a gentleman, a mysterious high-ranking individual, whose position, responsibilities – God knows what they were – made it impossible for him to spend more than those isolated weeks with her. I also knew that Flora did not suffer unduly as a result, and this friendship – alas, not purely platonic, of that there could be no doubt – would have presented not the least threat to my prospects had I had the ghost of a chance.

Flora would return with new outfits, new stories, a new hairstyle, new hats. She had that *joie de vivre* that made one forget her age, or made it seem a matter of secondary importance. Each day that she returned was for me the happiest day of the year. I would ride out to meet the coach and when I saw it appear in the distance across the plain, drawn by its eight horses, my heart would quicken as though I were once again a boy of fifteen.

However, it is not our story that I set out to tell, but the story of Flora and another. This other person appeared on the scene at the beginning of the summer of 1833, probably in June since one of the first memories I have of that young man is of him eating cherries, standing by a window in the home of Artemise d'Aubec.

IN ANGOULÊME THE DRAWING-ROOM of the prefect's house looks out over the Place d'Armes. The gates of the best inn in town open onto the square, as do the entrance to the town hall and the windows of the houses belonging to the town's most eminent personalities. It is also where the four main roads – to Poitiers, Périgueux, La Rochelle and Bordeaux – meet and circle the square but do not cross it. The Place d'Armes is a pleasure ground reserved for the local inhabitants. It is surrounded by the most superb plane trees which lend shade to a few green wooden benches that are arranged in pleasing symmetry. The cries of children are respectfully muted here, the townspeople walk more sedately, and in the centre of the square is the finest bandstand in the region – some say, the whole of France. Covered with sheets of reddish copper verdigrised by the weather, the roof is supported by slender but sturdy wrought-iron columns on which vines and creepers of bronze are most beautifully entwined. Its marble floor shows no sign of wear, yet it has resounded with the foot-tapping of thousands of polished shoes. Three steps lead up to this platform, three more in the centre lead to the stand occupied by the conductor of the Angoulême Orchestra. Without inviting comparison with the Philharmonic Orchestra at Covent Garden, as Artemise d'Aubec was wont to say, to everyone's amusement, the music they played was not at all bad, even if more sophisticated critics thought it rather unambitious.

That day Flora and I were returning from a most enjoyable fishing expedition, made even more enjoyable by the fact that we were late for our rendezvous with the others at Artemise's house. The Angoulême Orchestra was playing a waltz, a Rossini waltz – actually a Rossini tune that the tax collector from Cognac had turned into a waltz. The people in this part of the world love spending their leisure time doing something completely different from their work. It was the tax collector who arranged and conducted all our Sunday concerts. Despite his efforts, he had not quite succeeded in completely destroying Rossini, so it was to the accompaniment of delightful music that we entered the prefect's home. And since I was three paces behind Flora and was not, therefore, subject to the battery of thirty pairs of eyes, I saw the newcomer before she did. 'Gildas Caussinade' was how the lady of the house introduced him to me, adding without pausing to draw breath, 'the son of our farmhand Caussinade, whom you must know'. I thought this explanation quite unnecessary, but the young man seemed not to mind at all.

Gildas was extremely handsome – at least, I thought him extraordinarily good-looking, which surprised me as I had never noticed good looks in a man before. He had, I later discovered, only just turned twenty-three. His mane of hair was dark brown, almost black, his teeth were a brilliant white, and there was an air of refinement, something decidedly aristocratic, about his features, his bearing and his gestures. Even I found his youth and masculinity attractive, and they must have been irresistible to women. He shook my hand warmly, and assured me that his father – of whom he spoke without the slightest condescension, but on the contrary with every mark of respect – regarded me as the best notary in the neighbourhood since the occasion when I had acted on his behalf. And he seemed to share his father's gratitude towards me. When he smiled his eyes crinkled, his thin face relaxed completely, and he seemed the very embodiment of youth. He was charming and I was charmed, as were all the men present that day, when the truth was we should have done better to reach for our weapons and set upon him . . .

Flora had greeted all her friends and was making her way to where Artemise and I were standing. The young man, whom Artemise held firmly by the elbow, had his back to her. Artemise only released his elbow to tug at the sleeve of his rather tightly fitting jacket, which I recognised with the eye of a long-time resident of Angoulême as having come from 'Jeannot the Farmworker', who did indeed supply the agricultural workers in the region rather than the habitual guests of this house. She pulled vigorously at his sleeve with the intention of introducing him to Flora. He turned round, and all I could see then was the back of his neck. Beyond him, I saw Flora's face as she set eyes on him for the first time. I was interested to observe her reaction. I expected to see admiration in those features I had so often gazed upon and so deeply cherished – features I now found easy to interpret. I expected to see surprise at the sight of this beauty, so animal-like in its refinement, so refined in its virility. However, contrary to all my expectations, and those of Artemise – she was obviously scrutinising Flora's reactions as closely as she had observed those of all her guests – Flora looked bored and cold and resentful. It was not at all an expression she customarily adopted. And since Artemise had just introduced Gildas to her, as tactlessly as when she presented him to me, one might have thought it a sign of snobbish arrogance in this woman to whom both attitudes were quite alien. It seemed that her expression might be a response to Artemise's words: 'You know the son of our farmhand, old Caussinade?' But then a second later, when the grossly patronising and familiar tone of our dear hostess had worked its magic, the cloud of Flora's unfriendliness completely evaporated.

Flora held out her hand and spoke.

'Good heavens!' she said. 'Wasn't it you I saw the day before yesterday in the field just past the road to Porte? A field full of wheat, or something like that?'

'Yes, we do work that land,' the young man said, quite unabashed, 'but it actually belongs to Count d'Aubec. I think it must be thirty years now that my father has been working that land for the Count.'

'Then it must be you to whom I owe an apology,' said Flora. 'My mare bolted that day, and carried me across that field right through the crops. I was intending to come by and explain, and to pay for the damage, but . . .'

'It was nothing. Don't give it another thought,' said the young man. 'Your mare is very light on her feet. She's a lovely dainty creature. I replanted the seedlings this morning and you wouldn't know anything had happened. Count d'Aubec won't even notice. However . . .'

He paused, raising his eyebrows mysteriously, and leaned towards us. Instinctively, we leaned towards him, as if there was a danger of being overheard. But Artemise, to her great chagrin, had to leave us, and rush to the door to welcome an old Justice of the Peace and his wife.

'However . . .' Flora prompted him impatiently.

'These caused me a great deal more trouble than the field,' said the youth, suddenly exposing his hands. Until that moment he had kept them hidden behind his back, affecting a bourgeois stance, and now he displayed before us his calloused hands obviously used to daily physical labour, with swollen joints and broken nails.

They were strong weathered hands made muscular by so much heavy work. Beside them, mine, tanned though they were by hunting and riding and so on, nevertheless looked like the hands of a city-dweller. His hands were certainly much older-looking than his face; a man's hands, not those of a young boy, and Flora instantly averted her eyes with a haste that I, like a fool, attributed to pity or embarrassment.

'You've worked them to the bone . . .' she said gently.

'I was especially ashamed of coming into this room with the hands of a labourer . . . My presence is already quite out of place as it is,' the young man continued with that same happy smile of pride, that mixture of kindness and unconcern which suddenly gave me the impression that he was very content to be a peasant. (Had his handsomeness been accompanied by a title, it would no doubt have made him the most arrogant of young aristocrats.)

'Why out of place?' asked Flora without looking at him, her eyes fixed instead on Artemise, who was bearing down on us once again. 'I was given to understand when I was in England that in France all human beings were treated alike; indeed, that they were fashioned out of the same clay. I thought there had even been a revolution in this country to prove it.'

'That doesn't alter the fact that my name is Caussinade,' said Gildas with great gentleness, and with an unexpected trace of consolation in his voice. 'And that my father, my grandfather, and their fathers before them were labourers, and only worked on land belonging to others . . . We are a family of labourers. And what is more, we are the best in the region. Is that not true, Mr Lomont?' he added with a laugh.

'You are absolutely right. I can testify to that,' I said loudly, affecting a tone I adopted when surprised by the directness of a question, and which made Flora laugh.

Artemise, who had returned breathless but with her voice unimpaired, was already cutting in. 'My dear Flora,' she said, speaking through her nose, 'I introduced this fine young man to you, but I didn't explain why he is here.'

'There's no need,' said Flora coldly. 'The gentleman's presence is sufficiently agreeable to make any further explanation unnecessary.'

'Can you imagine,' Artemise continued, 'thanks to the offices of our good school-teacher, this young Apollo has already won a scholarship, or a prize, or God knows what extravagance the state offers young people these days, and now he has also passed I don't know which examination exactly, quite by himself, and he is much the most learned man here – certainly more learned than you, my dear Lomont, and much more learned than Honoré, but that doesn't signify a great deal. And what's more, do you know, this young man is a writer?' (She was speaking directly to Flora.) 'And his poems, instead of wasting away in Angoulême, have reached the capital and are even published in the *Paris Review*. Well, as Honoré said so amusingly, it's the first time for centuries the Caussinades have managed to surprise us in this way!' And there she concluded, having contrived to suggest that the Caussinades' status as farm labourers dated from the time of the Crusades, and by implication so did her own recently acquired minor title.

I DON'T KNOW WHY, BUT my memory of that afternoon is in colour. The weather was fine, as I have said, and the sinking sun shone through the French windows onto Flora's back, setting her hair ablaze, throwing her face into shadow and imparting to her eyes a subtle and dangerously becoming brilliancy. She wore a blue dress, the blue of rhododendrons, that was set off to perfection by Gildas's dark corduroy suit. It was a wonderful sight, I thought, the folds of pale watery blue worn by this woman in the full bloom of her beauty, in the summer of her years; and beside her, the thin straight figure in black corduroy, who gave no hint of the fevered and dangerous passions that must surely have pulsed in his young veins. Artemise and I lagged behind in aesthetic terms: I in my brown suit, she in the yellow taffeta she mistakenly thought was dazzling.

There was something magical in the air that day. Fate often seems to offer periods of repose before a crisis overtakes you and casts you down. Often in life there are peaceful clearings where all – lovers, rivals, torturers and victims – can rest together in friendly co-existence, oblivious of the hellish journey that lies ahead.

'My God,' said Flora emphatically – such outspokenness was typical of her, and would no doubt have caused critics to smile and even to describe Flora as a bluestocking – 'my God, Mr Caussinade, how I envy you!'

'But naturally, we *all* envy him . . .' said Artemise with good-natured indulgence, and she even sealed her words with a laugh. She glanced at me with amusement, as if to say, 'Dear Flora! Envy a farmworker – only she and the birds would do that.'

She must have seen in my eyes what I was thinking because she abruptly turned away and swept off in a fury to talk to other less romantic but more sensible souls.

'Artemise's sudden departure is very welcome,' said Flora. 'While she was here, I really would not have dared to ask you to recite some of your verses to us, right now . . .'

'But I couldn't,' said Gildas reddening.

'Please,' said Flora. 'I would very much like to hear them. Really, it would give me such pleasure.'

Only Flora de Margelasse would have dared to speak to such a young man so seriously and so innocently of what would give her pleasure. He must have realised this, and he considered her with equal seriousness, abandoning for a moment the cheerful but distant politeness that seemed to control his features. I saw him clench his jaw before he agreed, saying quietly, 'Very well, since you want me to, I will.' Then Flora smiled at him. She smiled at him, but with her eyes, in a way she had never smiled at me. For though there was respect and gratitude in those eyes when they met mine, I had never seen in them the fear, the defiance, the unease that I saw in them now.

So clear and infectious were these emotions that the young man turned towards the French windows to escape scrutiny. Flora and I immediately turned to flank him, while he drummed his fingers on the glass, trying to recall some verses.

As I beheld the grey square gilded by the sun, I was suddenly reminded of my childhood. I seemed to see myself as a small boy in a red smock, running after another little boy in black: I was boxing his ears, or maybe he was boxing mine, to the melodious sound of the Angoulême Orchestra and the indignant cries of our respective mothers. It suddenly struck me that this badly paved square with its young rascals – of whom I had been one – was my real birthplace. That was where I belonged, and not at all on this balcony beside a woman who was breaking my heart, and a young man reciting poetry to her. What was I doing amongst these people – they were not yet old, but they were certainly no longer children. I had no place in the company of these adults. I wanted to play marbles or tussle with someone my own age.

'That boy will never grow up,' my mother used to say. And no doubt my late development could be explained by her death just a few years later. Only now, for the first time in my life perhaps, did I truly miss her – her warmth, the smell of childhood that used to surround her, and the rough fabric of her housecoat on which I would lay my head when I was small. I regretted that her passing had meant so little to me at the time. Had she lived longer, I should have been better able to mourn her.

Young Caussinade's voice suddenly reached my ears, a voice thick with emotion, passionate but gloomy, a disembodied voice which emanated from a face turned towards the end of the balcony:

'When I see the flush spread to your eyelids,
When I see your lashes close on the misty seas

of eyes half-open on a dream of stone,
When I see your hand on the crumpled sheet . . .'

He spoke well. His voice was heavy and intimate, and after my initial embarrassment, I found it pleasurable to listen to him. I had never liked poetry as much as was fashionable at the time, but although I took no interest in it I could be moved by it. I was susceptible to its rhythms. Every day, Flora would remark on my aptitude for the music of poetry. If we were in the company of other people, I would laugh loudly, but, alas, alone in my room, I would swagger with pride.

There were occasions in my life when I would withdraw from the world, from contact with others, for just a few minutes or for hours at a time. And sometimes, with the aid of dreams, or books, or nothing at all, I would force myself to recognise the truth and resign myself to my physical isolation. I would not allow my poor bleeding heart to entertain the comfortless joys of a libertine. I resisted the temptation to believe that, if I could once possess Flora, my love for her would be quenched for ever. I would not lie to myself. I rejected vanity, the desire to be happy and to rest my pride and my wounds, all in the name of an uncompromising truth. For this examination of conscience, I even remember abandoning on the spur of the moment, without making my excuses, tables of feverishly excited whist-players, sofas buzzing with gaiety, and even those dinners *al fresco* that I loved – in the garden, when the women's dresses would stand out white and pale in the mysterious and sweet-smelling darkness by the time dinner was ended. I remember leaving a thousand warm and friendly places just to be alone . . .

Well, I assure you, I certainly succeeded in that. I am all alone now. Outside my study there is no one waiting for me with whom I could try out a few variations on the role I play, the stereotype of an honest provincial notary, a rich, selfish and secretive lawyer. There is no one for whom I could portray the sad and moving character of an unhappy and lonely sixty-year-old man.

That is the trouble, it seems, with tackling the past on the pretext of gaining a better understanding of the present – a present in which no one is interested, anyway. In dealing with the matter of dates and times, and embarking on mad forays and sentimental pilgrimages into the past, one inevitably invites comparison between then and now. There is no avoiding the bitterly painful questions about today. The voice of the present gradually drowns the already meaningless echo of the past. It is no use my trying to prevent it – the question 'What was I doing then, that Sunday morning, as I woke up?' automatically leads to another: 'And what are you doing now, this minute?'

What has become of the man who, when he was thirty, was happy to go riding with friends, and would sit proudly on his horse in fields and clearings, leaning down to rest his head against the beast's neck in the copses and woods of Charente? He has become that man there, full of shame, who is writing down his most intimate, most nostalgic thoughts. He watches in horror as morning and evening pass by, indistinguishable one from the other. He is repelled and terrified by those new machines drawn by iron horses noisy enough to herald the end of the world. He detests progress and the future as much as his past and his failures. His solitude is his despair, but his face never betrays him, and nor does his voice. He has no one to whom he can unburden himself, no one with whom he can laugh. And for the past thirty years, he would abandon family, friends, and mistresses, to be alone, to think in solitude. Is that not the most devastating irony?

I return to my balcony, with Flora and Gildas, whom I see once more standing close to one another, looking into each other's eyes and talking. The next time I saw them together, only a little later, the damage had been done, and so comprehensively that it seemed no one could be unaware of it. But I, the rebuffed lover, was the first to know that another's love would not go unrequited.

For two weeks no one spoke of Gildas Caussinade, and he was not seen in Angoulême. I thought I saw him one evening, as darkness fell, driving his father's plough behind two oxen, cutting furrows in the big field near the river. In fact, I did see him, very clearly, and I told Flora only that I thought I had seen him. I lied to her as I lie to myself today on this sheet of white paper – and still I do not know why.

On reflection, I think there were two reasons. One, which I did not acknowledge to myself, was my determination not to remind Flora of the existence of this over-handsome young man with literary pretensions. The other was a kind of remorse, because I had certainly seen Gildas Caussinade, stooped over, applying his weight to the ploughshare, with back bent and muscles straining beneath his coarsely woven shirt, in the servile attitude that had been his family's for generations. And I felt, to my surprise, an uneasy sense of satisfaction, not without an element of malice – a sentiment I detest, especially in myself. For as I sat on my fine chestnut-gold horse, leather riding-crop in hand, my silk shirt and ruffle fluttering in the breeze, and the supple leather of my boots squeaking against the saddle, I watched the young man working, and I could hear my own voice speaking, sarcastic and offhand, a voice that was already describing this meeting to Flora:

'I saw our friend the peasant-poet just a little while ago, my dear, casting his verses and sonnets into some very deep furrows. I hope they grow as well and as abundantly as the wheat in our rich, old earth . . . I must say, working in the fields suits that boy well. He seemed much happier and more at ease than he was in Artemise's drawing-room.'

This voice horrified me, as did the facile nature of my joke. I did not recognise myself. And, in fact, it was not I who spoke in this way, but a future Lomont, a future version of myself that I would one day come to resemble very closely. It would be a day of rage and despair, and destiny, wilful as ever, was now giving me a foretaste of it.

It was no doubt for these two reasons that I told Flora I thought I had seen Gildas, and not that I had indeed seen him.

Nevertheless, it is true that I forgot about him and thought Flora had forgotten him too. One day, after a picnic, we went looking for mushrooms with d'Orty, one of the suspected conquerers of the prefect's wife, who was now paying court, with a great deal less success, to the unyielding Flora. Flora and I found ourselves alone together, lying – almost – in the grass behind a thicket, while he roamed the woods plaintively calling her name – 'Flora! Flora!'

Flora despised him. And it was her custom, a custom now so rare, especially in our society, to shun what she despised. So we saw him pass by in his lovely wine-red suit and disappear behind a tree. Flora lay back, her hands behind her head, with that perfect tranquillity which the presence and the quality of my love imparted to her.

Her hair lay spread on the grass that was already tinged with russet. The sun turned her blue eyes almost green. Her neck was lightly tanned by riding and walking in the open air, and this made her look younger than ever. Her teeth gleamed between her lips, and once more I was disgusted by the thought that the love she inspired in me should be of exactly that kind which prevented me from throwing myself on her. So as not to have to look at her any more, I too lay back, my hands behind my head, like her, and closed my eyes.

As if the preceding scene were imprinted on my eyelids, Flora's face kept appearing, fading away and then returning in all her glorious young beauty. She had also closed her eyes, at least I sensed that she had since only a woman with her eyes closed would have spoken as she did then. For hers was a dreamy voice stirred by its own music, by turns rough and sensuous, a voice that must have been Flora's in bed, at night, with a man, a voice which murmured:

'When I see your lashes close on the misty seas
of eyes half-open on a dream of stone . . .'

She said no more. I lay there paralysed. My heart stopped beating. I dared not open my eyes. I was afraid to stay beside her, or even to look at her, because I feared that every fibre of my being must betray the awful, jealous, bestial wrath which overwhelmed me. She must have realised in the middle of the poem that I would recognise it, and she had not known whether to stop immediately or continue to the end. The intensity of my silence and the stiffening of my body may perhaps have alerted her, but too late. I did not utter a word nor move an inch until she had stolen silently away; until I had convinced myself with reasoned and sensible arguments that her reciting by heart a poem by Gildas Caussinade was not the shattering revelation I knew it to be.

A few days later, however, having buried this ridiculous incident in false oblivion – and when I say 'ridiculous' it is my own reaction I am describing – I learned from Artemise that Gildas Caussinade had gone to Paris in secret. As far as I was concerned, his secret was safe with me for as long as possible.

There followed two weeks of happiness. You may remember, it rained for ten days continuously, that summer of 1833. The following week was all the more sunny, and the sun all the more conciliatory since it had played truant for so long. Its liquid rays, warm and gold and pink, fell unstintingly on the white wheat and the fresh green trees and meadows, and on the houses and animals washed by the rain. They shone down on swollen rivers, on a countryside glazed with sheets of water, engorged with moisture and fresh streams. The sound of horses' hoofs no longer rang out loud and clear but was absorbed by the sodden ground.

A kind of languor was mingled with these downpours. How can I explain it? One no longer galloped, one floated. It seemed as though the outcome of the conflict between sun and water was uncertain, and therefore exquisite. A liquid veil, like a spider's web, interposed itself everywhere, muting voices, softening profiles, making gestures more slow, hearts more tender, complexions more gentle. Women's faces glowed with kindness and purity; men were less rough; and the willows wept more than usual. In short, Flora was kinder to me.

We would gallop together, eat together, talk and laugh together, and I would sulk alone, but so rarely one might have thought we were newly wed, and that her refusal to take any notice of my solitary brooding, merely acknowledging it with a smile more generous than usual, was almost part of a game. In two weeks there were only three occasions when I told her what was closest to my heart: that I loved her, that I wanted her, and that my life was of no consequence without her.

The first time, it happened almost by chance, in d'Orty's hunting lodge: we met in a corridor and tried to pass each other, she with her arms full of flowers, I encumbered with a brace of pheasants. We stepped to right and left simultaneously, clumsily barring each other's way three times in quick succession. When these antics were over, there was little distance between us as we stood there laughing and embarrassed – at least this was true of Flora. I saw embarrassment give way to panic in her eyes when, carried away by what I thought to be the most sincere, most honourable and most irresistible expression of my nature, I asked her to love me, not to shun me any more. Yes, I remember quite clearly saying to her: 'Love me, Flora. Stop all this and love me.'

She could not look me in the eye. She opened her mouth to speak and I do not know to this day what she might have said – I am still trying to pretend I have not the slightest inkling – if the pompous voice of the prefect had not called out from behind me: 'Well, then, Lomont, so that's how you woo your ladies, is it? Like a stable boy?' And I made my escape.

The second time was more premeditated, and also more cruel. She had been so deliciously, so unaffectedly tender and attentive towards me all day long, a whole day spent picnicking by the river Arce, that I went home to change for dinner in a state of ecstasy.

Yet I felt wretched because I could not tell her of my happiness, of my senseless, desperate gratitude towards her . . . And when I saw my rapturously enthusiastic face in the mirror, a face rounded and made boyish, indeed foolish, with happiness, and when I recognised it as my own, as the face of Lomont, the quiet little notary from Angoulême, I decided I had to find some reason why this stranger should exist.

I decided quite rationally to do the most irrational thing I could ever have done in the circumstances: I resolved to ask Flora if she loved me – as if, were it true, I could possibly have been unaware of the fact. I foolishly imagined that my question would dispel some mysterious constraint which was preventing this widow from freely confessing to a man madly in love with her (and he had made no secret of the fact) that his love was reciprocated. No matter. With the desperate optimism of those in love, I behaved as if this constraint existed.

I dressed, tidied my hair, put on my boots, and set out for Margelasse. Hardly had I dismounted than, holding my two gloves in my left hand, I was already in the blue drawing-room on bended knee.

Flora, thank God, was alone, and my arrival, my impulsiveness and the pose I adopted caused her to raise her eyebrows in stunned disbelief. For once, I looked on her without the advantage of my height, my knee resting heavily on the old splintered parquet floor. As I looked up at her, I could see the soft fragile skin of her neck. (No hunter, however bloodthirsty, can harden his heart against his victim's vulnerability when it is thus exposed.) I noticed the almost imperceptible slackening of the flesh on her jaw, the beginnings of what would later become a wrinkle. I desperately wanted to see that happen, I wanted to see time ravage her face, a sign that I would be Flora's lifelong companion, and a witness to her ageing. I observed the way her fine blonde hair curled round her ear; I noted the ear's sensual lobe, and the firm beautiful neck, graceful as a statue's. I gazed on this face like an aesthete, a predator, a drunkard, and an idolater. Then I met the bewilderment in her eyes, and without a single word, I rose, retraced my steps across the drawing-room, and galloped back down the avenue.

I ought to have taken to heart those wordless scenes in books which always mark a turning point; silence in love is more eloquent than any speeches. (It seems to me that all too often our lyrical writers fail to recognise this.)

Four days later I was waltzing with Flora in d'Orty's ballroom – a dance at which, by the most unlikely good fortune, I excelled. As I danced, my body, released from its bulk and weight, became light, as if inspired by unsuspected Viennese blood. My head was as intoxicated as my body, and the repetition of the three beats of the music perhaps seeming to justify the repetition of my declaration, I leaned forward to speak in Flora's ear. As usual when she was truly enjoying herself, Flora was disquietingly lovely. The tempo of the music was echoed within me – 'One-two-three, I love you, I love you, one-two-three' – and I told Flora what was running through my mind. My arm around her waist held her body close to mine, and the violins' voluptuous exuberance excited in her and in myself an equally voluptuous shiver of excitement that would have been odious to her had she hated me. Our physical closeness, the seductiveness of the music, and the heat of our bodies made this sensual *frisson* inevitable, but the pleasure I derived from it was deceptively innocent. In a word, I behaved like a stablehand, and when I caught sight of Flora's reflection in a mirror behind her, I saw her bared shoulders suddenly flush red with embarrassment.

Those then were the only setbacks to my happiness during those two joyous weeks. And I say that without any irony, for all in all those were the only occasions when I forced suffering on myself – when I tried to woo Flora. The rest of the time – meticulous notary that I was, the person who transformed into detailed records all the little comings and goings of human existence – I gave no further evidence of the most frenzied emotions I had ever experienced. Unruffled, I simply existed. Meadows, fragrant lime teas taken on terraces, rivers, ball-gowns and waltzes – everything had a dreamlike quality. Nothing disturbed my equanimity – neither those limpid eyes, the caress of her hair, and her peach-like cheeks, nor those hands held tightly in the shadows and my own uncertainty.

Those fourteen happy days might have lasted as many years and my body and senses would not have been any more alert when, like a clap of thunder, like an unexpected flash of lightning, Gildas Caussinade reappeared one fine evening in the middle of a ball, his forehead bloodied by a wound.

His entrance was sudden. The orchestra missed two beats, the dancers skipped two steps, and the hearts of most of the ladies quickened, so tragically handsome did he look in the candlelight. The orchestra stopped playing. There was a melodramatic silence and for a moment I felt an almost uncontrollable urge to laugh. However, though my jealousy had turned to curiosity, indeed almost sympathy towards this exhausted and breathless young man, the emotions he inspired in me were no laughing matter.

'I beg your pardon,' he said, in a surprisingly firm voice for one so pale, and he was clearly addressing Flora rather than the lady of the house. I watched her. Flora was whiter than I had ever seen her, even whiter than when her horse bolted one stormy day and covered five miles before she managed to regain control.

News had reached us of fighting in the streets of Paris, and Gildas was beseiged with questions. The music did not resume until later, and it was without doubt the most successful ball of the season, or rather the one that was generally considered the most successful, because it had been entertaining, and among the other pleasures it afforded, there had been an element of the unexpected. Only a person in love, as I was, or someone who had been a widow living in rural England, as Flora had, could have actually enjoyed the balls that took place in Angoulême that summer of 1833. Indeed, my love and Flora's insouciance are integral to this story. Nothing that is here related, nothing that took place, none of this mess, this disaster, this catastrophe, would have been possible had there not been, to start with, the dual loneliness of Flora and myself.

Flora's distress and pallor at the sight of the young man put me in a terrible mood. I accompanied her back to Margelasse, driving her tandem harnessed with Hellio, Flora's black trotter, a superb Irish gelding that was always frisky, and my Philemon, the ginger horse that Flora made me buy at Confolens one market-day. From the moment we set out I let the horses have their head, contrary to my usual practice, and if Flora had been unaware of it before then, she now realised what mood I was in. She tried to improve my spirits, warning me not to destroy her 'visky' as she still lightheartedly referred to her trap. Usually I would jokingly reprove her for this, and her other puzzling anglicisms, which must have numbered no more than two or three. This time I did not respond and she fell into a thoughtful silence.

I collected my own thoughts – or tried to. For suddenly it seemed that all my five senses, as well as my reason, my imagination and my memory were fired by the prospect of intensifying my suffering. Consumed with jealousy, and eager to feed this passion with anything that might encourage it, I felt as if I had grown an extra pair of eyes in my temples, enabling me to see more than I should; my ears seemed to develop tentacles to amplify my suspicions; while my nostrils flared to sniff out cause for further despair. All at once, it seemed that concealed beneath the façade of the carefree debonnaire young man I was thought to be, lurked a sick and sinister madman, cunning and perverted, intent on his own destruction. It was the first time this idea of being divorced from myself had occurred to me. And prompted by the outrage, the disgust and the fear that this sensation inspired in me, I urged the horses on, shouting at them, and giving them rein. They shied, sensing my anger immediately, and then raced into the darkness. During the ten minutes that followed we did not exchange a single word, so preoccupied was I in trying to regain control of the runaway horses.

After ten minutes – ten minutes of taking bends at an angle of forty-five degrees, hurtling over ditches and ploughing through fields – I managed to stop them. I jumped down and went to them, and having tethered them to a tree, I spoke soothingly to them. I patted their necks, and assured them of my affection and my regret; in short, I did for the horses what Flora should have done for me.

She too had descended from the tandem and was standing by me near the tree, her face scarcely showing any change of colour. Not a single cry had escaped her throughout this mad cavalcade, and her courage, which the day before would have won my admiration, was this evening a source of irritation. I looked up. There was a superb moon in the dark blue sky dotted with stars; but from time to time countless clouds – dark stormy clouds from the east, from the direction of Quercy – floated past the still moon. The muscles in my throat were tense as I watched them, my head thrown back, breathing with difficulty; my hands, covered with the horses' saliva and foam, rested against my fine new breeches, a pair of nankeen breeches that Flora had also encouraged me to buy one impulsive day. And in that instant the thought of all those unnecessary purchases, the roughness of the reins between my fingers and the certainty of my rejected love, everything, seemed all at once derisory and dismal.

'Nicholas . . .' I heard Flora's voice say and I lowered my eyes to look at her. We exchanged a peculiar smile – it has just come back to me now – a smile that seemed already resigned to what was to follow . . .

But my resignation was short-lived – I was soon tortured once more by doubt and anxiety.

YESTERDAY FOR THE FIRST TIME since I put pen to paper I had the feeling I was remembering something new, that I was rediscovering a memory that had not, until then, formed part of the fund of memories I carried in my head. I confess that this was a disagreeable sensation; I was even a little terrified. For I fear the sweetness as much as the brutality of these unknown remembrances lodged in my memory. Will the recollection of moments of happiness give birth to new regrets, and will bad memories yield new sorrows? What on earth drove me to open this notebook? And what tenacity or exquisite pain is it that keeps drawing me back to it – draws my hand to it even now?

I am alone, here at the window of my attic, where I have erected my ivory tower – as Monsieur de Vigny so patronisingly describes it. It is an ivory tower that smells of damp, and my loyal housekeeper despairs of me whenever I lock myself away in it. She believes I come here to work, and is shocked by the strangeness of the place. She cannot understand why I no longer use the fine mahogany secretaire that she polishes every morning. If she only knew what work it is I do . . . The scandal of 1835 may be in the past now, but the memory of it remains and does not fade. More than seventy miles away from Angoulême, people still talk of it.

Through the skylight in the attic I can see the evening approach. Across the lawns stretch the shadows of my house, my trees, of everything I own and for so long dreamed of sharing with Flora. I have since grown to hate these possessions because they have never become 'ours' but always remained 'mine': my house, my lawns, my heart. All but my heart have only ever known one single master. I have been denied the opportunity to make any gift of these things or to share them with another. Not for me the sweet words 'we' and 'our'.

The meadows are purple with autumn crocuses shimmering in the dusk. I can hear the church bells ringing, signalling an east wind and rain. When Flora could hear them at Margelasse, it was a sign of good weather. The wind always blew from different directions for the two of us – it carried different messages for her and for me. It is very stupid of me to be at all surprised that we never married.

The wound on Gildas's forehead was not the only souvenir he brought back from Paris. He also came with copies of the *Revue des Deux Mondes* in which his poetry had been published. Moreover, he had written a play, about which he was extremely reticent, and his reticence almost cost him very dear.

One day in the week after the ball, I arrived on foot at Flora's house. My horse had worked up a lather that afternoon and I was leading the animal to give him a chance to cool down. There was no one about so I tethered the horse myself and, without being announced, made my way towards the blue drawing-room, where I expected to find Flora, since she spent most of her time there. I stopped for a second in front of the cheval-glass to tidy my hair, and it was then that my whole world fell to pieces.

Through the half-open door I heard the voice of Gildas: 'I love you to distraction. I care nothing for the rest of the world, nor for the anger of your family. I care nothing for anything that is not you.'

He spoke in a feverish voice that was adolescent and virile, and with a conviction that made me murderous. I took two steps towards the door to that scene of sacrilege. My hand was on the hunting-knife I usually carried in my belt to cut away branches, to trim saddle girths, to pick stones from my horse's hoofs, and not, as anyone might have thought who had seen me that day, to cut a man's throat. In a single movement my hand had instinctively reached for that hitherto harmless knife, and held it in front of me, the blade bared and thirsty for blood.

'Can it be true that you love me? What wonderful confession is this! And I am as madly in love with you, waiting only for you to speak.'

It was Flora's voice, but she spoke these words haltingly, in a murmur. I realised only a moment before hurtling myself into the room that she was reading. It dawned on me just in time. I stood rooted to the spot and heard her laugh, a delicious, pure and tranquil sound that put me to shame.

'Your handwriting is quite impossible to read, Gildas!'

He laughed in turn, and even I was smiling as I entered the room.

'What are these declarations of love that can be heard even in the garden?' I asked with good-humoured ease which surprised Flora but seemed not to please the young man. 'My dear friend, I had no idea you were such an accomplished actress,' I went on, kissing her hand, while she glanced searchingly at me. This suddenly gave her an air of deceit that offended me. I felt superior to the situation, almost disdainful of what might have taken place. I felt indifferent, bold, reckless, and indeed I had all the recklessness, boldness and indifference that you might experience on discovering that you have escaped what could have been a fatal accident. Suddenly the river is no longer frightening, nor the idea of drowning. You think you are safe from the water for ever, and you step back smiling, unharmed and scornful, only to fall into the chasm that has opened up behind.

I realise now that I was, at least until I knew Flora, a person who had never really questioned himself – like so many men of my generation, and women too, perhaps. Only poets were expected to indulge in that kind of introspection, and those internal dialogues; and perhaps to take revenge for their isolation, they have misrepresented us. At any rate, they do not speak for us – no one does. My generation straddled two eras: one in which everything was forbidden and, as a result, everything was desirable and dangerously seductive; and another in which so many things were freely attainable and seemed dull as a consequence. These two eras have one thing in common: as far as one can anticipate, and for as long as there is life, no matter how often the cycle is repeated, both eras will always remain a subject of heated debate and endless speculation. Though society is confused by its own codes of conduct, it nevertheless continues to impose them. And poets, whatever they are like, will always be envied their freedom of expression. Our bourgeois decorum and our pathetic eagerness to conform will never silence the need – passionately felt by all human beings – to cry out loud, to scream without restraint as I am doing at this moment.

We are, we have been, we shall be . . . Why should I write 'we' all the time? Is it a last ludicrous attempt to reject my solitude, to deny the singular impotence of my life? I have always been gagged; I am now, and I shall die that way, a slave to laws and prejudices, customs and practices, fads and comforts, prohibitions and chains, without ever having known the reason for their existence, nor their origin, nor purpose. The men and women of our age have been brought up to despise one another, but to behave as if this were not the case. All of us who wished or hoped to abide by different rules, and not to play this supposedly normal and delightful game of love, have sometimes been scoffed at, or made outcasts. However, it is our less exciting and more common fate to have been imprisoned for life with a stranger. Neither the sacramental blessing of such an arrangement, nor society's approval, nor the innocence of the children who might result from it, make it any less hateful, poisonous and desperate to those caught in its snare. We are prepared for struggle, for confrontation, never for a union; not even for that friendship or trust which can be the consequence of or a substitute for passion. This will always make of us either uncaring despots, masters of women whom we do not desire, or victims of women of another kind, who appeal to the beast in us, and those take vengeance on us for their sisters, without even being aware of what they do, by a sort of natural justice, or perhaps simply because they are flirtatious.

It is growing dark. The trees no longer extend their shadows. A light mist presaging nightfall casts a veil over the meadows.

My narrative has not developed in quite the usual way this evening, and if I have a reader, and that reader has been patient enough to bear with the tortuous detours of my unhappy love story, he might perhaps feel he has cause for complaint . . .

I have, after all, decided to continue my account of what happened, but I realise that while I may not have mastered the skills of my more illustrious fellow writers, I have nevertheless made their faults my own. Re-reading what I have written, I can see all too clearly how readily I have succumbed to the shameful pleasure of fancying myself an illuminator of the soul. Here am I, the notary of Angoulême, expertly drawing the portrait of a heart I was unable to move, except to pity. Here am I explaining, analysing, pronouncing, proclaiming, identifying all the subtleties that have supposedly escaped the attention of others. As I go over my manuscript and see how far my native silliness has already progressed, encouraged by literary pretension, when I observe what flourishes my pen delights in elaborating, I suddenly experience an overwhelming sympathy for those men of letters against whom I have so often railed all my life.

I shall lay to rest on my feather pillow this heavy head inebriated by its own rantings. It would seem to be high time . . .

I HAVE TOO MANY VIVID memories, but since I have decided to recall the whole story, omitting nothing, let me then think back.

I can see myself still, standing in the hall while Gildas speaks words of love to Flora, whom I know to be not totally innocent. There I am, a dagger in my hand, ready to kill and revile a young man and a young woman neither of whom are in any way answerable to me. I tremble in every limb, I am drenched in acrid sweat, and I am obliged to support myself on an armchair covered in yellow damask. Perhaps when I die I shall again see that little antechamber to the large drawing-room at Margelasse. Countless specks of dust dance in the gold and ochre sunrays which filter through the closed blinds. The fabric covering the chair is faded. One of Flora's ancestors gazes down at me from the wall with a loathsome air of amusement. There is mud on the toe of my boot which offends and worries me.

I am a loser, ridiculously lost.

For the scene I had just interrupted may well have

been a rehearsal for a play, but it was also a rehearsal of the future, into which I was being forced to look. I remember drawing myself up, reeling, and catching a glimpse of my face in the mirror. The sight of it disgusted me, and the thought of the crime I should have committed tempted me once more.

I remember observing those two equally charming people a little later, and the pleasure they took in each other's company was already a torment to me. They had continued their reading and, no doubt spurred on by her audience, Flora's delivery was more fluent. She spoke those words with a greater conviction in the presence of a man whom this ring of truth plunged into despair. It was thanks to me, on that day at least, that Flora and Gildas were able to conclude their impassioned dialogue without too much difficulty.

As this thought occurred to me, a nervous and sarcastic laugh that I did not recognise as my own escaped me. The laughter was a relief and at the same time stabbed me like a sword. It was in this manner that I came to know myself. I discovered in myself a witness of my plight, a reader of my own story. I looked on my state of turmoil with clouded, cold and sightless eyes; gradually, over the years, all other expressions have been denied me. As I have said before, since Gildas came between Flora and me, I had experienced with increasing frequency mixed feelings that I could neither identify nor define. Their significance remained elusive, and I was unable to judge whether they were right or wrong. I had always considered myself an honest and reasonably courageous man. Now, more and more often, I felt myself to be cowardly, weak and dishonest – above all, cowardly. I would look away when I caught sight of myself in a mirror, and once, having brought my horse to drink from a pool of water, I disturbed the water with my hand to clear it of my

70

reflection. I did this without thinking, quite clinically, and it was only the freezing coldness of the water on my fingers that made me aware of what I had done, and what it signified.

'But you have nothing to be ashamed of,' I stammered, 'you have done nothing wrong.' And suddenly I realised that, alone in a clearing with my horse, I was talking to myself.

I SLEPT VERY BADLY LAST night and I believe I know why. This childish prattling about the past must be brought to a speedy conclusion. It is not in my nature to be demonstrative or affected, and I cannot therefore indulge any further this ridiculous confession. I will burn it at the end of the week.

That evening, while conversing on the lawn at Margelasse, I learned more details of Gildas's trip to the capital. It was his good fortune that he had encountered Monsieur Musset, and that his poems found favour with Musset. For once not prey to the petty jealousies of his profession, when confronted with another writer's talent Musset was delighted. I will say nothing here of Gildas Caussinade's writings. Basically I am no judge. I really admire and respect only documents executed and authenticated by lawyers – precise, cold perhaps, but trustworthy. Men are feeble-minded animals, always at the mercy of pride, anger, or lust. The most that one can aspire to in life is to subdue these passions, classify them, label them neatly and lock them away in drawers – this is the work of my profession and there can be little doubt it is one of the most useful in our society.

Gildas Caussinade, then, sealed the success of his verses with the Parisian public by his appearances, which completed the conquest of his already enthusiastic readers. He was fêted and lionised, and I am bound to say that he returned from Paris as if none of this had taken place. He came back as if he had never been applauded at the Café de Paris, as if Madame Sand herself had not proclaimed him a handsome young man. Gildas Caussinade came back like the peasant-farmer's son that he was, took up his pitchfork and harrow, and no doubt would have said nothing about his adventure in the capital had not Artemise and d'Orty, subscribers to all the Parisian reviews, spread the word. He was plucked from the fields, his hay-making and his cattle, and set down in the middle of a salon. His pitchfork was exchanged for a harp and his straw hat for a halo: the halo, irresistible at that time, of poetry. Of the conflict, the conspiracy perhaps, or the barricades from which he returned with the wound on his forehead, no one knew a thing.

Even today I do not know what Gildas Caussinade thought of all this. For a young man who tilled our lands, and expended his youth, his time, and his energies – observed all the while by our disdainful and ungrateful selves – to make fertile fields from which he would not harvest a single grain, there must have been a certain irony in seeing all these elegant people flocking around him, anxious to relieve him of his scythe when only a month before they would have been scandalised to see him lay it down for five minutes. I ascribed to him, I wished on him, the most bitter and scornful reflections. But he presented to my unfailing attention the guileless eyes of a puppy, or of a sensitive young man as innocent as he was idealistic. He was always smiling – even his eyes would smile – and I still did not realise – I absolutely refused to admit – that his easy manner and charm reflected the complete and utter indifference towards others of a man happy in love – or who thinks he is about to be so.

Flora too was enraptured, I could see it in her eyes, and she would quite openly recite the poems that had been on her lips on that picnic which took place not so very long ago.

Monsieur Jules Janin, on his way to see a relative in Nimes, did us the honour of passing through our good town, and rushed to embrace Gildas, who was the cause of his detour. The honour was reflected on each and every one of us.

There were dinners where naivety vied with pedantry in the most shameless and ridiculous fashion, and it seemed no one was aware of it except myself – I, smouldering, devastated, impotent, furious, good old Lomont, debonnaire and affable, notary by profession. This transformation from the friendly sheepdog I used to be into a poisonous snake must have been undetectable since it escaped even Flora's notice. But, after all, she no longer noticed anything that concerned me. She would address me without actually talking to me, she would look at me without seeing me, listen to me without hearing what I said. I believe I could have kissed her and taken her, and she would not have felt my touch. I did not have the courage to try. Gildas did it instead of me, and perhaps proved that I was wrong.

One evening when it was once again pouring with rain – in fact it was the first time it rained that brilliant autumn, although it seemed to me there had been one long deluge since the return of the poet – because of the weather, Gildas found himself in the position of accompanying Flora back to Margelasse alone. Having drunk a little Toquay wine or some champagne – an unusual occurrence because the boy did not drink – he dared to say to Flora what she had been waiting for him to say. She let him speak. She let him bend his fine dark head over her in the back of the carriage, and allowed his burning lips to explore her body. She let him accompany her up the steps of her little château, and climb the staircase to her room. She let him into her bed, beneath the billowing white sheets I had once chanced to glimpse and whose image haunted my nights – and haunts them still . . .

This summary of events so horrifies me even today that I have just broken my pen and a splinter has lodged itself under the nail of my index finger. This is the reason why I am stopping here. I shall go on with my story some other time – if I go on with it at all . . .

A MONTH AGO I DECIDED to abandon this account and even to burn these pages. But I could not do it, either because I have succumbed to a weakness said to be common to all scribblers and become attached to my own prose, or – and this strikes me as the most likely explanation – because the habits of a conscientious lawyer will not countenance any unfinished business. So I shall continue, but I must try to be less bitter. For it is true, alas, that recourse to sarcasm proves almost inevitable when a man speaks of a woman who has not yielded to him. He is harder on her than a man who has been satisfied, even if the lover is afterwards deceived or rejected. However cruel memories of carnal pleasure may be to the victim of passion, nevertheless he must feel some tenderness towards his tormentor, and it is this tenderness that the spurned suitor is denied, no matter how vivid his imagination. For the scent, the warmth and the flesh of a woman create in the memory a bed of infinitely greater sweetness than the most ardent desire is capable of conjuring up, if passion finds no release. Gildas, were he still alive, would speak more kindly of Flora, although he did not love her as much as I. He would speak more gently and more respectfully than I, who seem to judge her and even to despise her . . .

Flora, my Flora . . . My heart, my soul, my beauty, my sun! My only fire . . . The only laughter in my life . . . Ah, if that is true, Flora my beloved, if alone in the earth where your destruction is completed, in the night to which you have escaped me for good, you have discerned in what I have said anything that might be interpreted as an insult, forgive me . . . Forgive me, for you know I weep for you every night . . .

To return to my story: it took place thirty years ago, I remember, and thirty years ago, the erosion of what are now described as prejudices – but in fact were simply the instinct for survival amongst our upper classes – had scarcely begun. Good society conformed – and ostracised those who flouted convention.

Flora was born a Margelasse; her ancestors (on her father's side) had joined the first and second Crusades, and her mother could trace her ancestry back to 1450. But however far back Gildas Caussinade traced his origins, his family had always been not only commoners but peasants, and even further back in the past, serfs. All his ancestors had been servants to our ancestors – and to us, his new friends, he still doffed his cap when he spoke. Gildas Caussinade could never escape this. Despite being a poet in Paris, he was every day in danger of being whipped, or worse still, tipped, should one of his 'friends' happen to be in a bad mood.

You can well imagine: it was impossible that the friend, the lover, the companion of Flora de Margelasse should endure that – the coin or the whip. It was equally unthinkable that those self-satisfied squires should from one day to the next address him first as a farm labourer and then as a gentleman. And moreover, if they were to start calling him 'sir', it would be impossible to say whether it was amusement or insolence which prompted them.

Did the two lovers give the matter any thought? Had it even occurred to them? I would swear the answer was no, however strange that may seem. Neither one nor the other had for a single moment dared hope their love would be shared. As far as we the onlookers were concerned, the distance which separated them seemed enormous, but to them, aware only of their own feelings, it was virtually insuperable. They heard only the sound of their own heartbeats, and each feared that the other would remain deaf to their love and have no word to say to them. In short, they must have woken up the next day more amazed than horrified, and not so much horrified as happy: the grey immutable sky of their existence, of their unrelieved loneliness, had just been torn asunder and in the rent had appeared a brilliant radiant sun, the sun of a love shared. What did it matter that behind the sun the storm clouds were gathering, the urgent, menacing clouds of scandal? They were quite unperturbed. And yet Flora was inviting her ruin, exile from her natural environment, disgrace and loneliness in old age; while Gildas invited insults, anger, hatred. But I repeat once more, neither one of them had time to consider all these things, or if they did, it was as if the dangers were unreal, so unreal as to be almost desirable. Neither of them was frightened by any other prospect than that which already drove them to despair every evening: silk sheets or a straw mattress, what difference did it make? . . . but empty, horribly empty in either case, when each of them had a nightly rendezvous with solitude and a hopeless nostalgia for the body of the other. This emptiness, this hopelessness and this nostalgia, indeed this desire, are all that we three had in common. But in nothing was I gratified nor appeased.

It was in October or November, I no longer remember, that I was summoned to Bordeaux to give evidence on behalf of an old fellow student facing trial. He was a small landowner blighted by misfortune in all things: disinherited by his family after having failed at college, he was then robbed by his neighbours. Finally, unable to bear his wife's infidelity, he had killed her. I went to Bordeaux and when I realised how incompetent his defence counsel was, I virtually took over the case myself. I did not do too badly, and in the end saved his neck from both judge and jury (the neck he himself slipped into a noose, however, two years later). It was my good fortune to bring tears to the eyes of the ladies and to please the journalists who had come down from Paris to observe a spectacle now rare: a gentleman being tried for a poor man's crime, a man of breeding jealous of his own wife. These journalists also shed tears at the trial, encouraged a little by the local wine, and they sang my praises so that I returned to Angoulême in triumph.

I travelled seventy-five miles in eight hours, changed horses three times, and arrived at Margelasse in a state of exhaustion, without forewarning anyone of my visit. In my foolishness I believed that the angels of fame, having blown their trumpets in the precincts of the court in Bordeaux, had wasted no time in flying off to play the same anthem in Flora's ears and that all Aquitaine echoed with the sound of my name and news of my return. It was the second time that I had arrived somewhere without warning, and it was to be the last. The old aunt who had raised me, and taught me the golden rule never to call on anyone unexpectedly and without giving due notice, would have no further cause to reproach me and could henceforward rest peacefully in her grave.

Anyway, hardly had I reached Angoulême than the driving energy that had spurred me on, leaping from one horse to another during those seventy-five miles, suddenly evaporated, and all at once I succumbed to the fatigue of that journey completed in such youthful haste. I was shattered. I could no longer feel the bit in Philemon's mouth, which I had been so relieved to recognise only an hour before. I was no longer able to adapt myself to his pace, which was very swift after three days' rest. I rode him badly, vexed him, and when we arrived at the gates of Margelasse, to the disgrace of his rider, he was drenched in sweat. I decided to let him dry off a little, dismounted and walked alongside him up the avenue. I too was drenched, and should have preferred to be like my horse, sweating with fury and not with fear, as in fact I was, without knowing why. I was gripped by a sense of foreboding.

But I say again, I had triumphed, my ears were still ringing with the praises heaped upon me in Bordeaux, and my humour improved as did my horse's. This splendid beast was no doubt saying to himself, 'Now then, let's not get excited. My master is clumsy today, but after all he is not cruel. He doesn't use a whip or spurs. Let's be tolerant.' And I was thinking, 'Now then, let's not get excited. Flora is impulsive, enamoured of poetry, but she is not lacking in discretion. She has a sense of decorum, and self-respect. Of course nothing will have happened.'

I hoped to find Flora alone at Margelasse, without her gallant admirer. That a woman of noble birth should have desired him to read his poems and expressed her

81

appreciation of them could not have allowed a Caussinade to forget that she was still a noblewoman. If I were to tell Flora of my suspicions, she would laugh in my face. And I could not help smiling as I remounted, imagining, already hearing, the tenderly mocking voice of my Flora.

Philemon, once more proud and happy, cantered into the courtyard and I only just managed to stop him at the fence: he would willingly have scaled the steps, anticipating my own plan.

TOTAL SILENCE REIGNED IN THE garden that early afternoon. The sky was a blue-tinged white on the tiled roof, a hot dust-free sky without a breath of wind, where a still storm lay in wait.

I walked round the house to the right, loath to retrace the abhorrent path I had taken on my last untimely visit, reluctant to traverse that yellow hall. I hoped to find Flora on the verandah that overlooked the lawn to the west, where she must be feeding her swans, or reading poetry. I was sure I should find her there, as it was her usual retreat when the weather was fine. And I really believed I should find her there alone – I swear it. Just as I swear that I still do not know what caused me to tread so softly, so carefully, on the crunching gravel, and so furtively on the red-tinged lawn. I thought nothing, I wondered at nothing, I feared nothing, I desired nothing. I felt drained. I was sweating and felt suddenly bereft. The person creeping about like a spy was a man I did not know, and he no more knew what to expect than I did. The proof is that this stranger was thunderstruck when he rounded the corner of the building and saw Flora leaning back in her cane armchair, Gildas lying at her feet with his head on her lap. She had just taken a strawberry from a dish to her right and was trying to slip it between the young man's white teeth. But he was clenching his jaw, laughing deep in his throat, and she was insisting, also laughing, pressing those slender, pale fingers against Gildas's full and swollen lips, which were, I could tell, warm and urgent. Flora's fingers lingered there, trailing over his mouth before wandering up to his forehead, and slipping into his hair. And the palm of her hand was left at the mercy of that gentle mouth. His lips parted in the very centre of her palm and kissed it again and again while Flora closed her eyes and ran her finger-nails through his hair. I did not move a muscle while all this was going on, petrified as I was with fear. Yes, I admit it, today I admit it – it was fear: the ignoble fear of being seen, the fear of being caught spying, of being obliged to behave like someone who has seen – that is to say, to behave like a man incensed, outraged, contemptuous, a man whose duty and sense of honour would keep him henceforth at a distance from Flora, since Flora de Margelasse was conducting an affair which, if not against human nature, went against the social order, and she had chosen to abandon herself to the former rather than observe the latter. My whole life had taught me to prefer the very thing she flouted: order.

I began to walk slowly backwards, step by step, trembling lest they should see me, trembling at the thought of retreating in this manner. What had happened to my fury and the desire to kill Gildas that had consumed me the month before? Who was this prudish, troubled man in the depths of despair, but fearful above all of confronting the full extent of his loneliness? Having reached the wall from whence I had come and behind which I disappeared, I leaned back exhausted against the stone. And there, dear reader, if you can bear any more of this, there I drew breath, I smiled and felt safe.

Safe? I had just lost every hope of happiness. I had seen Flora enthralled by another, captivated by another, at the mercy of another. Safe? I had seen Flora trail her fingers between her lover's lips and in her lover's hair, with all the languor and pleasure of a woman who has surrendered herself, who is loved and loves being loved. I had been unhappy for months already because I had not made her mine, and now I could no longer hope that she would ever be mine – now I could even imagine her possessed by another. Safe?

I staggered over to Philemon and leaned against his flank. I rested my head against his neck, and stood there motionless, my heart in my mouth. I saw him turn his head towards me. I saw with unseeing eyes the pearly white of his own surprised and shining eye; and as I imagine a drowning sailor clings to a raft, I clung to him, my horse, my only friend. I murmured his name, lovingly, ridiculously. And when he pulled on his bridle and nuzzled my burning face, distorted with emotion, with the cool velvet of his nostrils, tears sprang to my eyes. I pulled myself into the saddle heavily, clumsily, like an old man, and I let my beast return to its stable and take me back to my equally deserted room. There was no hurry, nor would there be ever again, for the rest of my life, since all happiness was dead.

I did not know it then but that was only the beginning of my sorrows. Nevertheless they already seemed very harsh. I returned to my study looking like death, and the congratulations and compliments my clerks and servants showered on me at first seemed insane, until I remembered that it was the success of the trial and not the rout of my emotions to which they paid homage. We drank champagne. I drank too much, like a stupid uncouth fool. And the wine combined with my exhaustion and despair almost had me rolling under the table at the feet of my secretaries. Pride or my sturdy constitution spared me that indignity, and I managed to climb the stairs to my room without falling over. There I collapsed onto my bed, sideways, impaled beneath the canopy and the family portraits by seventy-five miles on horseback, three bottles of white wine, and thirty years of loneliness. I slept deeply for twenty-four hours. By the time I awoke, everyone knew about the liaison between Flora and Gildas.

WHAT I HAVE JUST DESCRIBED and what took place between the two lovers, I learned from Gildas, the last night I saw him. His young face, suddenly that of a mature man, hopeless, and nearer to death than to his childhood, is before me still. Gildas's great attraction for men as well as women, it seemed, was his difficult rupture with adolescence. His healthy body was as straight and tall as a young tree; his gestures were often gauche, despite his innate grace – unlooked for in a product of the soil of Saintonge; and his eyes shone sometimes with a guilelessness that emphasised rather than detracted from the fiery vitality of his intelligence. For Gildas Caussinade was an intelligent young man. I had recognised that from the start, unwillingly, angrily and resentfully. For it is shameful to regret that one has not been able to despise someone. I was never able truly to depise Gildas, although it seemed he had given me every reason to do so. I hated him, I wished he were dead, I . . . Oh! I may as well admit it: above all, I envied him. I have never envied anyone as much as I have Gildas Caussinade, a peasant and farmhand, a labourer whom my housekeeper allowed in her kitchen only under sufferance. I envied this man, though I had never envied the most illustrious lawyer, or the richest landowner, or the greatest poet, or the most devout priest, or the most doting father, or the most cherished child. I had coveted nothing and envied no one, but merely to think of him, of her, of the surprise of their lovers' awakening in the bed at Margelasse, a kind of filthy lava floods over me, interposing itself between my eyes and this paper. If I were to cry, my tears would be black, or a foul yellow, or purple like the sap of certain trees when they are cut down too soon and which then exudes a nauseating odour.

They woke up surprised – he first of all, unprepared for the sight of those white sheets and his brown hand lying in that whiteness like an alien object; then she, puzzled by the warmth so close to her, by the heat of the body still touching hers, which in her drowsiness she had not yet realised was a body. He recognised the sheets, the bed; she recognised the origin of the warmth; and they turned to gaze at one another in wonder and fear.

'I was no longer sure of anything,' Gildas told me. 'I was afraid she would cry "Rape", that she would have me thrown out of the house and beaten, that I might have dreamed everything, or that she might have forgotten what had happened. I felt guilty of sacrilege, and at the same time I could still feel the exquisite pain in my shoulder where her teeth had sunk into me a few hours earlier.'

He did not tell me what Flora's thoughts were, but I could well imagine. With a woman's terrifying simplicity, that some of us men interpret as a sign of their lack of soul or intelligence or moral conscience, she had thought only that her dream was real, that her love was there, and that the whiteness of the sheets made his bronzed body even more seductive. She drew him to her without a word and gave herself to him with the same abandon, the same ardour that she had shown him the night before – and all night long.

Naturally this is not what Gildas told me. He said no more than, 'Fortunately she recognised me immediately', and stopped there, but there was a fleeting glimpse of perfect happiness in his expression, and his eyes closed on a memory of bliss which pierced my heart more surely than if he had allowed himself a less discreet description.

They remained in each other's arms until midday. There was a knock at the door and Flora's maids were growing anxious. Gildas wanted to disappear, to hide, to flee; he wanted to avoid compromising her, he told Flora in all honesty. He jumped out of bed, and while he dressed, he told her he could well understand that she would not wish to see him again, that she would wish to forget everything; he would ensure their paths never crossed, and no one should ever learn of what had been the most beautiful night of his life. He said his memory of it would remain with him for ever, as lasting as his silence. He would have continued in this vein, with his noble and heroic speech, if Flora had not burst out laughing and held out her arms to embrace him again, to tidy his hair, and arrange his collar – the collar of the only decent shirt in his poor man's wardrobe, which he had worn to the ball the previous evening. And while he spoke of society, of proprieties, of her reputation and the terrible consequences from which he wished to protect his mistress, she spoke to him of cambric, and styles of shirt, and the things she would buy him as soon as she went to Paris. The discrepancy between what each of them was saying finally struck them and they both stopped, looked at each other, and at last realised the full beauty and horror of their predicament.

Gildas fell silent. He stood there motionless, looking at his hands 'without seeing anything', he told me later, ready to leave, ready to kill himself, but also ready to stay. It seemed to him that an age had passed before Flora's voice reached him and he realised what she was saying to him in all seriousness – which was that she loved him; that she saw no cause for shame in this, but for happiness; that she would no more hide him than she would rob herself of him just when she knew that this happiness was shared. Gildas thought he had gone mad. But not for one moment did he think she was mad. There was something so reasonable, so true, so well balanced and gracious about Flora that the word madness seemed at complete odds with her personality.

'But you cannot . . .' he stammered, 'you cannot . . .'

She interrupted him, and called out to her maid to enter and bring them both breakfast.

'I had no will of my own,' Gildas went on in conclusion of his story. 'I had eyes and ears only for her. I would have hanged myself if she had asked me to, just as I would have made love to her on the Place d'Armes, or even in her buggy, in front of the whole of Angoulême.'

That is, in fact, more or less what she asked him to do – not to hang himself, of course, nor to make a public spectacle of their lovemaking, but she rode out with him all afternoon in that same buggy drawn by her black trotter, the faithful Hellio. They went along every street, every lane, and to every square in town. She stopped in front of every shop, held his arm wherever she bought anything, and greeted all her acquaintances still holding that arm with the matchless air of pride and submission of every woman in love when she walks beside the man she loves and he is her all.

Gildas moved as though in a trance, waving, bowing, tethering the horse, opening doors, climbing back into the carriage, helping Flora into it, setting off again, smiling at her, answering her questions without understanding a single word she said (and what is more, she confessed to him later, she had no notion of what she said either). The eyes of Angoulême, of its inhabitants, which had first of all reflected surprise when the afternoon began, then amazement, then fury, and finally the joys of a scandal, were filled with the most unadulterated hatred when Flora eventually decided to return to Margelasse, where the couple dined with healthy appetites. There was no talk between them (at least they did not discuss their afternoon). Then in full view of the dismayed and scandalised servants, they retired very early to spend a second sleepless night of love together.

Thereafter, for the next two days, they were not seen again in town – where they were, however, the only topic of conversation

I was subjected to innumerable accounts of their outing, of that shameless exhibition, and they all mirrored the righteous anger and resentment that any morally principled society must feel when its laws have not been observed. Flora was more censured for loving Gildas so openly than for loving him at all. It might have been possible to tolerate her wantonness, her taking him into her bed, but not her calmly strolling about on his arm in public. And although I would have dearly liked to share the outrage and anger of our town, because of a foolish sense of justice and despite my personal resentment, I could not despise what I considered to be Flora's courage, her strength of character, and her loyalty. I admired her. I hated her, of course, but I admired her.

On the other hand, the rest of them made me smile – the witnesses, the judges, the blusterers, all those who did not want to challenge Gildas, because, they said, they scorned this peasant unworthy of their swords, whereas, if truth be told, they were afraid of wrestling with him with their bare hands and being soundly beaten. In short, I despised all those who were prepared to insult Flora sooner than take revenge on her happiness.

As for me, I did not know what to do. Work was unbearable to me, not doing anything was killing me, grief was driving me mad. I went riding all the time, always galloping, always in the opposite direction from Margelasse. This seemed to go on for months; in fact, it continued for three days. At the end of those three days Flora's letter reached me in my study. It was five o'clock in the evening, and her letter contained only these few words: 'Come. I need you. Flora.' I went, I flew, and it was to find Flora and Gildas in the hall, dressed for a journey, their bags already stowed in the carriage. They were pale and handsome, beautiful at least in the happiness that was so insufferable to my eyes. They were leaving for Paris immediately.

Flora took my hand and raised her lovely tender eyes to mine. I gazed deeply into them with a despair too obvious no doubt, because she blinked and her voice trembled.

'Goodbye, my dear Lomont . . .' she said. 'I shall never forget you. And I only find it so hard to leave because of you. Goodbye, my friend, goodbye . . .'

I said nothing. I shook Gildas's hand distractedly, and retreated. Night had already fallen. Autumn had already set in, and it would be a long sad winter in

Angoulême, cold Angoulême, to which Flora would doubtless never return.

Two years passed. One day followed the next and they did not seem similar because I was bored. Contrary to common belief, when one's existence is completely uneventful, the days are quite distinct and different from one another, according to one's moods, one's humour, one's freedom from care. It is only when one is happy that the days seem the same. I know the truth of this, since the only dawns, the only evenings that I can still identify are those of that painfully happy fortnight which I described earlier, during that sumptuous summer when I was weak enough, foolish enough and had the wit to feel happy, profoundly happy in Flora's company. But I would be incapable of establishing a chronology for those two weeks, of arranging in sequence and putting a date on the thousand details, the thousand images which sometimes, as I fall asleep, still pass before an old man's eye.

It is dark in my room. I always keep a candle lit at night – I prefer the light it sheds to that of a gas lamp, and this is further evidence that I am an old man and belong to an earlier age – but now the candle fills my room with smoke and fouls the atmosphere, lending an air of tragedy to the bourgeois fittings and comforts. The coals in the grate cannot remove the chill from the air, which I have difficulty in breathing.

My flesh has shrunk; my body has lost its strength and grown old, bloodless, and white, with grey hair and dry skin. I cannot stop this body shivering, despite the eiderdowns my housekeeper piles on top of me. Although the mahogany chest of drawers, the mercury in the mirrors and the copper candlesticks gleam in the light of the dancing candle-flame as it catches them, every evening I feel poor, ruined, ill, on the threshold of death, and in an abyss of loneliness. This room becomes a hospice, this bed a pauper's pallet, and these sheets a shroud. I suck my teeth – teeth which now can chew only white meat and vegetables – and my eye-lids close on dull eyes; even in broad daylight, covered as they are with a thin film, a shadow can render me myopic or presbyopic, as medical jargon would have it – in any case, I can be blinded by day, and blind by night, fearful at dusk, distraught at dawn. And now, with those eyelids closed on dead orbs, I can neverthe-less see from behind them, skies of the bluest blue, leaves of the reddest red, countryside of handsome beauty, friends gaily cheerful. And I retreat, I stagger backwards, I stumble, I fall away from this exhausted and lonely body, I surrender to a whirlpool and let myself float and drift with the waves, with the wind, with all the suns. I let myself sink back into the past – only that particular past, those fourteen days, no others.

Flora on horseback ahead of me turns round, smiles, waits for me because my horse is lame. Flora looks at d'Orty who has just said something silly. Flora looks at me; she is trying not to laugh but can't help herself when she sees my face flushed red with the same effort. Flora is annoyed with me because I have taken a whip to my shying horse. Flora accuses me of being a brute. Flora forgives me. Flora inclines towards me so that I can forgive her for having to forgive me. Flora rests her gloved hand on the pommel of my saddle, next to my own bare hand, the hand of a man of law, a strong hand made to take her. My hand does not yet know that Flora will never lie beneath it and still believes it will one day explore her body, that her body will one day be mine. Already my hand imagines itself descending from her shoulder to her knee, and sees itself confident and skilful, so much longed for, so greatly desired. It is a hand more proud of her than of myself. My foolish hand defies reason, defies, above all, the evidence before my eyes, for I can see clearly, beneath the suede glove, another hand, which is calm and does not tremble on the reins, nor on the pommel of the saddle – Flora's hand.

Did that all happen on the same day – Flora so cross, my horse so wild, and I so brutal, then so repentant, and so uneasy? Was it at the start or at the end of those fourteen days? Did this episode mark the birth or the conclusion of my great affair, my only love story, my personal novel, my passion, the sublime sensual passion of Nicholas Lomont which reached its climax after fourteen days of outings and picnics in the company of a woman he did not so much as touch unless by chance?

Then I wake, once more my eyes open on the present. I am surprised and comforted by the fact that the candle is still burning, that I am still alive. It is a good while, a full minute, before my heart stops beating so fast, before I succumb to any thought of unhappiness at my continued existence when Flora's life is ended. And again I am saddened for a long time.

Then I begin to feel vaguely content, despite myself, and to feel warm in bed. I begin to breathe peacefully and to feel my pale thin blood pulsing through my fingertips. And I am happy for another moment until I am struck by a sudden fear of death, by the certainty of dying – my own imminent death and the thought of the unknown into which I shall be tossed. I am frightened by the prospect of the earth that knows no respect, and that coffin made of oak or fir wood – what use is wealth when it comes to this? I am terrified by that worse solitude, both blind and dark, to which I shall be abandoned without a second thought. Then my body will be at the mercy of the beasts and weeds, while my spirit perhaps is cast out, God knows where, into the blackness of the stars, shrieking with fear in a solitude beyond human understanding and beyond definition; and my terror-stricken soul searches for someone or something, seeing nothing, feeling nothing, knowing nothing but that it exists and is lost for ever, and for ever condemned to this nameless horror . . .

Then I leap up in my bed, pull the bell, and call my servants; those old women, the young chambermaids of the past, are roused. My housekeeper has become an old, very old cripple who comes running, wailing and panicking. They all rush to my door: ugly, grey, frightened, old – just like myself. They look at me with pity, fear and a dim sense of relief.

Flora . . . Flora . . . What has become of her? Perhaps she too is lost, and shrieks in the darkness? Perhaps she can even see me, unhappy Lomont, good old Lomont, poor Lomont? Perhaps at last she needs me?

I MUST CEASE THIS NARRATIVE. I had decided to stop as soon as I reached the end, or rather the beginning of that idyll between Flora and Gildas, and that once they had set off for Paris leaving me desolate and foolish as usual, watching them depart, I would then put down my pen and hide my notebook in a place where I knew it would remain hidden for ever.

But I could not do so. Hardly had I written the words 'It would be a long sad winter in Angoulême, cold Angoulême, to which Flora would doubtless never return' than my hand – instead of writing the words 'The End' and dating the manuscript, signing it, hiding all that I had written, and picking up my pen to deal once more with the deeds and documents with which it is more familiar – of its own accord, moved to the top of the next page and continued, independent of my wishes: 'Two years passed. One day followed the next and they did not seem similar . . .' As if I had never decided to arrest this hand or as if it had rebelled against me . . .

Oh, but what is the point of lying? What good will it

do? While it may give me a last opportunity to deceive myself, or torture myself, or afford me some pleasure, it cannot be denied that this notebook has become indispensable to me and, if I were not to write down the end of this story, I would not survive three months. For it was the end that gave me retribution, but left me destitute.

Until now I have written only of Flora's happiness and my own unhappiness. And while I cannot go on to describe any happiness of my own, which never materialised, I can at least tell of Flora's unhappiness, which was devastating. Although I am racked with pity and my heart grieves for her, yet there are moments of senile wickedness when her suffering salves some vile festering wound in me that I cannot bring myself to name. What man is base enough to rejoice in the despair of one he loves? But what man is high-minded enough to rejoice in the happiness of that same person when her happiness is shared with another man? But base or high-minded, good or bad, shame or happiness, what does it matter? All that is over now, and how badly it ended! Instead of spending the night rambling like an old woman, I shall waste no time in explaining exactly what happened, and the how and the why of it.

NOTHING WAS HEARD FROM THEM for two years, but during that time there were constant reports from Paris which marked so many steps in Gildas's fabulous progress towards fame. To give a brief account of those reports, I could do no better than to quote the following few extracts from the *Journal des Débats*.

3 January 1834
The audience at the Gymnasium yesterday gave an ovation to *The Silken Arrow*, a drama in verse by Monsieur Gildas Caussinade.

11 September 1834
The collection of poetry entitled *The Avenues of Melancholy* by Gildas Caussinade was this morning awarded the *Grand Prix* by the *Académie française*.

10 November 1834
In the course of the evening, our fine young poet, to the cheers of his admirers, including of course the

ravishingly beautiful Countess of Margelasse, was congratulated by the King himself.

30 November 1834
Monsieur Gildas Caussinade, by the grace of His Majesty, has been knighted.

And finally, *1 July 1835*
Sir Gildas Caussinade has left Paris for the provinces whence we hope he will return with another masterpiece. Our eminent young poet will no doubt visit his estate at Forchent, but he will probably be staying at the residence of the Countess of Margelasse.

These excerpts are taken from the *Journal des Débats*, a liberal but respected paper, one of the few that one can obtain in Angoulême and not be ashamed to be seen reading in public places. Indeed it is the only paper I made a habit of reading.

From time to time, and only in the less savoury pages of the gutter press, I would chance to learn of the drama of Flora's liaison with Gildas. Their passionate affair, at first scorned, denigrated, subjected to the caustic comments of those who resented their own provincial status, gradually, as success, honour and distinctions were heaped on Gildas, had become a love worthy of respect, beyond reproach, and was evidently so deep as to discourage the gossip columnists who revelled in drama and thrived on tears as others thrive on Médoc.

I was sitting then, with d'Orty, on the terrace of our favourite café on the Place d'Armes. We were waiting until it was time to cross the square to go and dine with our prefect and his lovely wife, Artemise. D'Orty's conversation, as I believe I have mentioned elsewhere, was anything but amusing. So on the pretext of checking the report on the stock exchange, I asked the waiter to bring us a copy of the *Journal des Débats*. I held it open in front of us so that we could both read it.

It was the beginning of summer, and the swallows dived low over the square, signalling rain, but that did not dampen our good mood. Although we were to go hunting the next day, we had, I think, drunk a couple of sherries too many – one gets so terribly bored in Angoulême if one is not working from morning to night. But it was a Saturday. Both of us being early risers, our want of something to do had led us too soon to the Café d'Aquitaine, and we had imbibed a little too much Spanish wine. My unfocused eyes skimmed over the articles held out before them – articles that described some bloody carnage in Poland, and some of those awful incidents brought about by the folly of mankind in Europe and elsewhere.

It was d'Orty who first noticed the only catastrophe which actually affected us. 'Well, well,' he said with that loud nasal laugh which he claimed had driven the women in Paris to distraction when he was twenty, and now that he was thirty-five still drove people to distraction, men as well as women, so vain and stupid was his awful laughter. There are people like him whose faults and defects one tolerates all one's life with unimaginable patience – patience of a kind one would never extend to any member of one's family, nor to a friend or loved one, but which nevertheless, it seems, is considered unexceptional and is taken for granted. I was therefore in no hurry to read the column in the *Journal des Débats* which had prompted this 'Well, well'. It was ten minutes before I so much as glanced at it, anticipating disappointment, but I was stunned:

> *'Our eminent young poet will visit the part of the country from which he comes, where he will no doubt stay at the residence of the Countess of Margelasse.'*

My glass seemed to dissolve in my hand and smashed to the ground, splattering a dark stain onto the white nankeen breeches of the unfortunate d'Orty, who jumped up cursing and swearing. Waiters were called for, hot water and ammonia applied to his garment; there were protestations, apologies and his absurd anger, all of which gave me the chance to compose myself and pass off the consequence of my distress as sheer clumsiness.

The swallows had regained their optimism when we crossed the square and they were soaring through the air with piercing cries of joy. Their shadows flitted across the walls and flagstones. But their song and trajectories seemed to me so many terrifying omens. Those were cries of anguish they uttered, and they were birds of prey whose shadows streaked across the sky.

After a copious and delicious meal, which despite all her shortcomings Artemise was nevertheless capable of organising, all these macabre thoughts seemed quite out of proportion. I was once more a man sound of body and sound of mind. Normally I ate well, could hold my drink and slept deeply, and the least failure in any of these activities would invariably cause me an almost metaphysical anxiety, a sense of foreboding that a wing of chicken could immediately dispel. It was no different from usual that day, and I remember that without the slightest discomfort I was able to announce quite casually to our hostess, for once less well informed than I, the imminent arrival of our celebrated lovers.

There were shrieks of amazement, of pleasure, almost of indignation, Oohs and Ahs, cries of 'It can't be true, no, it's not possible', of 'But that's unthinkable! How dare they? But what can they be thinking of?' – in short, a flood of countless questions to which there could be no reply.

It was her husband who was the first to display annoyance. 'I do not see what is so surprising, my dear,' he said. (This 'my dear', which she could not tolerate, was clear evidence of his annoyance, and silenced her immediately.) 'I do not see anything at all surprising in *Sir* Caussinade's desire,' he said with ironic emphasis, 'to visit his good parents. Nor is it surprising that the Countess Margelasse should return to the home of her ancestors . . . Really, I do not understand your amazement. What about you, Lomont? And you, d'Orty?'

'No, nor indeed do I,' d'Orty opined after a long moment's thought (marked by a deep frown, a pendulous lip and an even more pronounced air of stupidity than usual, so obvious was it that he was not engaged in thought at all). 'No, I do not understand it either, my dear Artemise. After all, it is their home . . .' he concluded ponderously. 'She's coming home, and he's coming home, to see his parents. She's coming home to Margelasse and he is staying with her, is he not?'

'And you, Nicholas, are you not shocked?'

'Good God, Madame,' I said coldly, or so I hoped, 'dear God, to the best of my knowledge neither one of them is an adulterer. Monsieur Caussinade is someone of whom we may be proud, and his social acceptability can surely no longer be questioned since the Queen herself receives him at Les Tuileries.'

Artemise gave me a strange look, in which I thought I detected a mixture of scorn, curiosity and, if indeed she were capable of it, compassion.

'Well, gentlemen, since you are so forgiving and tolerant,' she said shrugging her shoulders and raising her glass with a suggestive glance that she could not carry off, her neck being too thin and her nose too long, 'let us drink to our famous lovers. Whatever happens,' she concluded, emptying her champagne glass with a melodramatic flourish so that she bumped her nose on the rim, 'whatever happens, I shall not be the first to receive her in my house.'

'Of course not,' said Honoré with unexpected acuity, 'but you will be the first to visit her as soon as she extends an invitation.

'What time do we set off tomorrow, gentlemen? Do you know, Lomont, that a boar has been sighted . . .'

If I seem to be losing the thread of the story in irrelevant detail and appear slow in coming to the point, or more precisely to the two really vital characters at the heart of this tale – vital in the sense that they were the only ones who loved each other, who told each other of their love, and proved it every single day – it is because I am afraid of having allowed the reader to forget in the course of my account what was in effect both the background and the principal actor in the drama: the peaceful town of Angoulême.

Everything which follows is marked by blood and tears, by blows and embraces and screams; it is all black and red, and will darken the pale blue skies of that summer, and turn to ominous purple the gold that tints the houses and the dense pure greenness of the rivers. And this awesome and deadly drama, this fateful violence, will take place in a small provincial town set in a gentle undulating landscape such as Ronsard described, a town such as Carpaccio might have painted, with its plane trees, its pigeons, its little wrought-iron balconies, its streets, and its inhabitants who wallow in their dullness, their good manners, and their well-kept trivial secrets. If I describe as evidence of this the mindless stupidity of one, the double-edged affability of another, and the outright malevolence of a third, and relate their vacuous remarks, mentioning cramps in my stomach and the change that seemed to come over the swallows, it is to suggest to the reader – what am I saying? It is to clarify for myself, sole reader of my only work, the way in which all the protagonists of this story were trapped in a pattern of events they could not escape, that year in Angoulême. What I mean is that had they been in Paris, none of this might have happened, or things might have turned out differently. I mean that without those secrets and the necessity for secrecy, without those observances of proprieties and respectability, without the perpetual striving after esteem which constitutes the essence and the animating spirit of all our provinces, there might have been no deaths; there might perhaps have been none of this destruction, none of these still-smouldering ruins, not only in my memory but also in the memories of those few local people who witnessed the tragedy. In Paris, a dissolute place, the drama might perhaps have developed otherwise; it might have been lost, choked in the cesspits and sewers of the capital. The air here is too pure, the water and the sky too clear. If people are bedevilled by some passion, their eyes give them away; and if their passion flaunts itself, they become as if alienated from nature.

I went home after dinner laughing a little bitterly over my surprise and the broken glass. Whatever I might have said, I was still deeply sensitive to the fate of poor Flora de Margelasse, now mistress to her peasant-knight. Yet it was some time since I had given any thought to her existence, or the place she once held in my life. A year had passed before I ceased to think of her except on occasion, and although those occasions were numerous I had by now freed myself of her. I was no longer in love with Flora, which was a great pity for a man so little given to sentiment as I was. But at least I should have loved once in my life with some fervour, even if this fervour was set at naught. I had been free for two years, free of Flora, of my love for her, and the memory of her. And when I received a friendly note the following day, in which Flora asked to see me, I set off at a sedate pace on the old familiar route to Margelasse, smiling at the thought of the wild journeys I had made here in the past with my aching heart thumping against my ribs in time with the galloping of my horse. I was still smiling as I climbed the steps and greeted a new maid, a woman with an unfriendly face who had obviously been brought from Paris and who, without so much as glancing at me, and without asking my name, led me into the blue drawing-room. Even there, I continued to smile at the thought of how cruelly hurt I had been, and how jealous and enraged, one summer's day, an eternity ago.

I smiled no more, because Flora came into the room almost immediately. And when I left to return to Angoulême, I was in turmoil. I could hardly keep my seat on my horse. For I was still, and always would be, madly in love with this woman. And the swallows and their unseeing cries had been a warning I had not heeded . . .

I REMEMBER WRITING THOSE LAST words yesterday evening in a kind of harsh hate-filled spasm of remembrance. My memory was trying to recreate – but to no avail – the images of that catastrophic day. What other word but catastrophic can describe the feelings of a man who has loved in vain, and suffered in vain, in his pride and in his body; a man who thought the blind and pitiless wild dogs of his passion were dead and suddenly sees them lying in wait once more, panting, ravening, the whites of their sunken eyes gleaming in deep dark sockets, their fangs bared in a savage rictus. Having said that, I cannot remember a single word Flora said, nor a single gesture she made that afternoon. Does the left-luggage office that is our memory refuse, after a certain lapse of time, to release certain memories considered dangerous and suppressed by our instinct for survival? I do not know. I can only recall one pale fault, a single blue patch in the grey blanket of the sky, a ridiculous detail: the intolerable squeaking of my saddle as soon as we broke into a trot. I remember the ludicrous resolutions such as 'Berate the stableboy as soon as I get back', or 'Change my saddler', which so inappropriately punctuated my reflections on the enormous discovery that overwhelmed me, and made my train of thought absurd even to myself. 'What am I to do? I am just as much in love with her now as before . . . What shall I do? What is to become of me? There must be some kind of polish that will stop this leather squeaking. Go away, naturally, but where? Flora will be everywhere. And how am I to go anywhere with that terrible noise deafening me? – and so on. As if I had no other saddle, and instead had two occupations and two destinies to resolve.

As our prefect had foreseen, Flora had no sooner arrived than she announced her intention to hold a big party at Margelasse, a huge ball to which all of Angoulême and its neighbouring parts were invited. And the lover of the mistress of the house would of course be present. It seemed that nothing had changed except that if one were to insult Gildas Caussinade now, no one could deny him the right to demand satisfaction; it would be a challenge to the sovereign power. Our prefect was not sufficiently revolutionary nor was his title of such long standing to allow him to be so audacious, or to protect anyone else who might undertake the risk, had there been such a person. For it was not only a newly dubbed knight to whom any would-be swashbuckling hero would have to throw down the gauntlet, but also a new man. Gildas was no longer the virile but vulnerable young man we had known. He was now twenty-five years old, still slim and broad-shouldered, but his face was now in keeping with his body; it had not hardened, but it had developed an air of authority. His eyes retained their trustfulness, but had lost their ingenuousness; his enthusiasm had become more purposeful, and his deference towards us was now a mixture of innate courtesy and the manners he had learned. In short, it was a very distinguished-looking man worthy of every mark of respect who was received as Flora's guest that evening. And a man to whom, it was very obvious, she owed a new and touching, almost sorrowful beauty.

In contrast to him, everything in her was more fragile, more delicate. Everything hung on her love, a real and vital love – the handsome dark-haired man who was laughing over there with the coquettish and amusing Artemise. I was talking to Flora as he laughed, and I remember thinking that I could see beneath her diaphanous skin – so translucent that it made her seem almost insubstantial – the bright red blood whose sensual satisfaction had, thanks to Gildas, given a fullness to her lower lip, and increased the pulsing at her temples and her throat, and seemed to have drained the blood from her eyes: the whites of Flora's eyes were almost blue they were so white. She looked at everyone, myself included unfortunately, with a gaze pure as only the constant indulgence of her sensuality can give to a woman. She was so beautiful one wanted to kneel before her as much as have her lie beneath one's body. Her whole body had a lustre of carnal gratification that made the men at the ball now stand back, and now draw near, without their even being aware of it.

'They seem so happy it hurts to look at them,' was the sober verdict of the prefect when we left at dawn in my cab, one of their horses having become lame on the way there.

'Happy? You cannot be serious . . .' Artemise began, but Honoré d'Aubec was not to be talked down.

'They make a very handsome couple,' he said quite firmly, as though there were no more to be said. And after a pause, he asked me, 'Tell me, Lomont, do you know the girl who was serving lemonade at the buffet table?'

'Yes,' I said, 'she opened the door to me the other day. Her name is Martha. I imagine she comes from Paris.'

'Oh you think so, do you?' he said distractedly. 'I thought I recognised her.'

I was quite embarrassed by his question, not that amongst ourselves we men did not discuss our exploits with the girls from the local inns of whom we had shared experience, but to refer to them in his wife's presence seemed to me in the most appalling bad taste.

'What an absolutely fascinating conversation, my dear,' said Artemise, for once quite justified in interrupting, but as unsuccessful now as before, because without paying any attention to her, Honoré went on:

'What do you think of her, Lomont?'

Once again I was nonplussed, until I remembered that some of the men had been hovering around the buffet table all evening, while other more discerning guests, myself included, had devoted their attentions to Flora and her charms. All at once, I recalled the new maid's slender but vigorous and sturdy body, the luxuriant jet-black hair drawn back from her face, her grey cat-like eyes, her sullen provocative mouth. She was indeed a fine figure of a woman, and in the darkness of the cab I conveyed this opinion to Honoré by a discreet wink, man to man, which he did not acknowledge, for he became suddenly preoccupied with his vines, about which he began to complain, to Artemise's further dismay.

I should not have given this incident another moment's thought if on the following day, having applauded Flora's great beauty, her radiance, and her happiness – and their praise on all three counts was my despair – the men who had been guests that evening had not then contrived to turn the conversation some-how or other to this same creature. I realised with some amusement that on her own ground she had scored as great a success as her mistress. It must be said that a normal healthy man is more likely to become enamoured of the attainable than the totally in-accessible. And while Martha seemed available, Flora belonged only to Gildas. These men were not to know, no more was I, that while the chambermaid may have been available, even if they possessed her body, she was more completely and more tantalisingly in-accessible than ever Flora de Margelasse would be.

IN THE CHARENTE, THE SUMMER of 1835 was one of the most wonderful in living memory, even though I suffered the frenzy of a madman. Talented young people, musicians, men of letters, men of the world, gay gallants and pretty ladies travelled at least twenty times to and from Paris to spend a few days at Margelasse with Flora and her poet. We provincials, kindly and untutored country folk that we were, were nevertheless invited on each occasion to enjoy the intellectual delights of their sharp witticisms and their brilliant conversation . . .

I am ashamed of what I have just written. I am bitter and unjust. Gildas and Flora's friends were, after all, Parisians, and as such they were more light-hearted, more carefree, or more determined to appear so, than we were. But having seen how lively they were, how friendly and enthusiastic in their appreciation of all that was the pride of Aquitaine, only the sad austerity, the unrelenting bigotry of the most religiose ladies in the parish would have led one to detect in them the slightest hint of a life of depravity. Although the men might not always return the following week accompanied by the same lady as the week before, it was done discreetly and no comments were made; one drew no more attention to a new liaison than one did to the rupture of an earlier one. At the centre of this gaiety, of this uncomplicated way of living – and living happily, it seemed – Flora and Gildas were like the very embodiment of happiness. Not only in our eyes, not only for me, drunk with despair by the certainty of knowing them to be happy, but also in the eyes of their friends from Paris, who were visibly and unreservedly enchanted by the success and constancy of their union.

Overwhelmed as I was with work, two months passed during which – my conscientiousness as regards my professional duties being equalled only by the frivolity of my private life – I did not leave my study except to feast until dawn at Margelasse, at the d'Aubecs', at d'Orty's, or elsewhere. I slept little, and would wander in sunlit fields or in the pale light of dawn with the wide-open and owlish staring eyes that distinguish the miserable. I saw nothing. My life was a few faces: Flora's and Gildas's joined together in an unbreakable alliance; my clerk's, whose ugliness was a strange comfort to me; and the face now and then reflected in my mirror, when I had the courage and the time to glance into it. Only one incident worthy of mention occurred before the thunderbolt struck that suspended time and brought the years to a halt at the end of August.

One evening after dinner, a quiet dinner at Margelasse – we were only ten at table – Martha had just poured us the famous lemon juice served only at Margelasse, and d'Orty was complimenting her on it over and over again, when Flora exclaimed, 'Martha has hundreds of recipes like that, which she learned at home, curious recipes unknown in France – because her father is Italian and her mother is Hungarian!' She smiled affectionately at her maid, whose determinedly severe expression relaxed for a moment when she replied:

'No, Madame, it is the other way round.' Then she bowed and left the room.

'Of course! That's right. It is her father who is Hungarian and her mother is Italian,' Flora laughed. 'How silly of me to forget.'

'Yes,' said Gildas, who was standing behind me.

I turned, as did everyone present, so inappropriate to the occasion was the harshness of his voice. He was pale and looked suddenly angry.

'Yes,' he repeated, 'when one has the goodness to enquire after people's personal lives, one ought to have the goodness to remember what they tell you. After all, it was not the mating of a Shetland pony and a Barbary horse to which you were referring, but that of two human beings.'

We were shocked and aghast, and he must have sensed this for he then muttered 'Excuse me', bowed towards Flora, and went out into the garden.

Artemise – unusually for her – came to the rescue by quickly changing the subject. I turned to talk to Flora, who was sitting next to me, looking even paler than usual. Then I noticed for the first time a faint wrinkle beneath her lovely bright eyes that had been brought to the verge of tears by the insult she had suffered. And for a moment I hated Gildas with all my heart.

'How could he?' I whispered. 'How dare he?'

'But he is perfectly right,' Flora replied just as softly. 'He is quite right. I am the one who is rude and indelicate, with my false charity.'

I protested. Flora was renowned for her charity for miles around, and for her generosity and kindheartedness. It would be quite unfair to criticise as an affectation her visits to outlying villages, the countless instances of her attempts to help her less fortunate neighbours, her donations to schools, to hospitals, and the open house she kept at Margelasse. But even had her charitable works been mere ostentation, she nevertheless managed to bring relief and comfort to many, thereby enabling them to support an otherwise intolerable life. And for this reason Gildas's remark seemed to me cruel and unjust.

He was in the middle of writing a tragedy – and was unable to free his mind from it, as he himself admitted with an agitated and confused little smile when asked. In contrast with many of Flora's guests, Gildas never spoke of his writings, nor of his past successes, no more than he did of the works he planned to write, and of his future triumphs. In fact, despite my most determined endeavours, I could discern in him no cause for contempt. His outburst that evening, which was perhaps the first breach in a fortress it was my earnest desire to see in ruins, came as a disillusionment. And the following day it was without the slightest compunction that I spoke with scant civility to Artemise, who was thrilled by this incident, and which she explained in a manner that reflected very poorly on herself.

'What can you expect?' she said. 'Whatever people like that may do or say, they cannot escape their background. Arguing over a servant's parentage! Only a Caussinade knighted just two years ago would take such great exception to a mistake of that nature. Anyway, our friend Gildas will always be a peasant at heart, more concerned for the fortunes of the peasantry than for people like ourselves. There is no denying that.'

I silenced her by firmly reminding her that, as she herself had declared not long ago, the only true nobility was a nobility of spirit – with which for the moment she seemed not to have been greatly blessed.

Her reply was cool. We both took umbrage, and despite Honoré's attempts at conciliation, I left in a rage directed both towards her and myself.

Honoré had gone into a visible decline since the beginning of summer, and I had often seen him heading in the direction of Margelasse and returning thence looking wretched (as indeed did all the men in our circle who were drawn thither). It seemed that Martha was little impressed by our attempts to charm her, but she was, however, susceptible to those of the head coachman and d'Orty's second whipper-in. According to my housekeeper, who told me before I could stop her, Martha had several times been discovered with these men, naked in the sunshine, behaving like an animal.

I REALISE THAT I AM reluctant to relate what must follow. It is so monstrous and so defies human understanding that I fear for the protagonists who must be destroyed by it.

I have spoken of Flora's love for Gildas, a love that was open and touching, and I have not omitted to say in what measure that love was evidently reciprocated. No man has ever been more eager in his attentions, nor more tender, more respectful, or more responsive to a woman's needs than Gildas was with Flora. There was no woman in Aquitaine, or Paris, either, I imagine, who would not have wished to be loved in such a manner. He spoke of Flora as of a woman to whom he owed everything, including his talent and his career, while in truth he was indebted to her only for his happiness (not that this was inconsiderable). His gratitude towards her resembled that of a drowning man towards his rescuer, of a pupil towards his teacher, a lover towards his mistress. He never ceased to show his respect for her, he protected her, he cherished her, and his desire for her remained as constant and as exclusive as ever, or so

I thought. Thus, when I entered the alcove beyond the gun-room at Margelasse, I was prepared for anything but the spectacle that met my eyes that sun-red evening.

In that little square room were carelessly piled masks, foils, and rapiers belonging to defunct members of the de Margelasse family, and even a few hunting knives. I had come to fetch an Oriental dagger which Flora had been describing to us as we drank a glass of port under the plane trees. The engraving on the knife was apparently very fine. Had Gildas been there, he would have fetched it, but as he was probably busy writing, I went instead.

I opened the door on a room lit only by a loophole window, a room that smelled of rust and leather, and was musty, dusty and damp. In the corner I saw before me the infamous Martha, leaning against a saddle, her hair in disarray, her head thrown back, her teeth bared in an expression of animal pleasure. Her dress was up about her waist, her legs held apart by the hands of a man whose mouth was pressed hungrily to her right thigh, and whose rough voice I could hear indistinctly.

'I cannot live without you. You are mine, only mine. When? All my life, if you will. I beg you. I want you . . .'

And this voice would no doubt have continued its deaf pleas if, with eyes wide open, the woman had not caught sight of me and stiffened involuntarily in surprise. I could hardly see the man in that half-light – for the light from the window revealed only what I must own was the savagely beautiful face of the girl. All I saw were his shoulders, the nape of his neck, and a pale profile. When he slowly turned towards me, while his hands pulled down Martha's skirts, it was as if I had been struck across the face: the eyes that met mine belonged to Gildas. And I might have killed him there and then had I not noticed a smile that was horribly inviting steal over the girl's lips and over her immobile face.

I staggered out of the room, saddled my horse and galloped back to Nersac, unable to believe what I had seen, certainly incapable of braving Flora's unsuspecting gaze.

Apart from those involved, no one knew of this ghastly passion. No one except me. And no one, thank God, was less disposed to gossip than I. But the following day, we were to go hunting on the estate of the Marquis of Doillac, where I would meet Flora and Gildas. What should I say to them? And above all, what should I say to Flora? How could I bear to see her gazing the way she did at that perversion of nature, that fickle and faithless heart, Gildas, when the least such glance would have satisfied all my desires.

But what desire? I no longer felt the slightest desire. I felt only anguish at the thought of what Flora must suffer, and it seemed her suffering would be not long delayed. From beyond the hills I thought I could already hear the too loud and strident voice, coarsened by cruelty, of the Old Lady of Death; certainly it was a voice fit to issue orders, orders that one of us was to receive forthwith. The Old Lady was coming to Angoulême, bringing pain and tragedy in her wake.

But for once this Old Lady could not stifle in me the violent cries of that beautiful bird, the exquisite bird of hope. This hope revived now allowed me to imagine, as in some violent cartoon sequence, Gildas the Handsome killed in a field by my hand; Gildas dead at my feet, and Flora, her back turned on the sight of his body, clinging to my shoulder; Flora dazzled by my gallantry, and still trembling at the fateful outcome of our duel; Flora murmuring 'Without you, I was lost . . .'

From time to time I thought I could hear this phrase ringing in my bloodless ears, white as my face and body must have been. What should I say to Gildas tomorrow? What should I do to him? Should I challenge him, threaten him, insist on his breaking off this other liaison? How on earth could this man who was otherwise blameless make love to a chambermaid under the same roof as his mistress? And above all, how dared he speak to her those words of love that are reserved for other women, women of one's own class, women of virtue. If Gildas had been surprised by anyone other than myself he would already be a social outcast. Even if he were indeed physically obsessed with this harlot, what folly could have driven him to say such things to her? Why speak of love to a serving-girl who was the self-confessed conquest of two men: a coachman and a stableboy? She was the kind of woman a man takes once and pays her a few coins, a woman he can have again at will, for the same price, and whom he can forget even more easily at no cost at all. Why these words of love? Words she obviously found laughable, for I was under no illusion as to the import of her smile – of that I was ever more certain. 'People like that,' Artemise would say, 'people like that do not know the meaning of decent behaviour.'

I was asleep as soon as my head touched the pillow. That was the only control I could exercise over my mind, and probably its only chance of survival: faced with the most deeply vexing problems, I would obliterate them by sleeping if I could see no solution to them.

It rained all night and the rising sun was just visible through wisps of mist that hovered a few feet above the ground, clinging to hedgerows, gradually disappearing amongst the trees, and fading away to reveal in the first light of dawn a still-slumbering virgin landscape.

All men, whatever their status, their age, their disposition, have, at some time or other, celebrated a secret, sensual and primordial union with the earth. Suddenly the round earth is theirs – their wife, their mistress, their death. We have all on occasion rendered thanks to the mud and the rain for having given birth to us, and for having allowed us, for however short a time, to walk through the mists, the fires, the silken sheets and the thorn bushes of the rain-washed countryside and towns now drying in the sun.

That morning the first rays of sunshine made the earth steam in the early freshness of the day, and the poplars further away in the distance stood nonchalantly to attention, as always. I had to stop and gaze at the valley. Bathed in the silvery blue, yellow or white of its sparkling dews, all at once this countryside seemed to me like an enormous cake, magnificent and inedible.

I was late arriving at the meet. I followed a whipper-in, and found myself at the head of the chase urged on by the mournful baying of the dogs, whose cries, for once, deafened me. I was the first to reach the boar at bay. I cut its throat myself.

Opinions varied as to whether I had brought the chase to a conclusion that was swift and splendid, or one that was sad and squalid. It is true that for a long while I felt I was pursuing my own death, and flirting with the risk of dying, but all the time I was merely tracking an exhausted boar that was cunning and aggressive, and no doubt as unhappy as I. I must confess that for fifteen minutes my only thought had been to kill him – as if his name were Gildas.

AFTER THIS STRANGE EXECUTION, DEVOID of any finesse if not of a certain courage, I felt better. Those birds that stirred sang in harmony with the bird of hope that was mine once more. At last it had returned, bringing light and joy to my life after two years' absence, two years' gloom and discomfort in the sun by day, and fiery cold by night, two emotionless years without bitterness and without intemperance – for my very modest indiscretions could hardly be considered intemperate. From time to time I would visit Bordeaux when I could no longer deny the demands of my body and my emotions. I went to forget my sentimental dreams, or at least to try to; I would at once surrender to graceless whores, and conceal from them, the tender landscapes of my nights.

It was while riding along an avenue at walking pace that I suddenly realised that the next time I went to Bordeaux I should ask for a girl who resembled that creature Martha – if she was not already waiting for me when I arrived. I do not know why, I had harboured the memory of the whiteness of her white thigh, and the brilliance of her grey eyes. I day-dreamed about her for a good fifteen minutes, and I must have fallen asleep, because I awoke a little later, entwined in her arms in a room in the Louvre where Louis XIII slept; I could hear rain falling on the roof. For the king's ransom I was prepared to pay, she kissed my neck, my shoulder, my thigh. This ridiculous dream infuriated me, and I urged my horse to a canter. Then to a gallop. Suddenly I was happy. I cannot deny it. I was happy. The clouds, the mists were no longer imprisoned by hedgerows, they were receding, dispersing in the sky, and seemed now and then to bounce against invisible obstacles from which they hurtled away, driven along by the same strong frolicsome wind that must animate the nightbirds of the capital, the revellers, the good companions of Gildas and a Parisian Flora I did not know. In short, all at once I felt very cheerful and very alert, as if delivered from my mad love affair, my story-book passion.

Without properly visualising it, I had imagined there would be some kind of scene when we met again, when we were brought together in our three new roles: the mistress betrayed, the faithless lover, and he who had witnessed the betrayal. I had imagined Flora melancholy, yet she was laughing gaily. But most of all, I had imagined Gildas awkward, pale and shifty, and instead I found him laughing with her, and his laughter was in no way diminished by the sight of me. On the contrary, I thought I could detect some sense of irony in his dark eyes and his handsome open face. The hearty laugh that escaped his too-white teeth, Flora's uneasy glance at his splendid mouth, and the shadow that darkened her amethyst eyes kindled in me a desire to kill him, to strike the face of this living lie, this wretch, this scoundrel, this underling, who had not only inveigled his way into the bed of a noblewoman but dared to be faithless to her under her own roof. It was I who must have turned pale because Flora left the tree against which she had been leaning, surrounded by admirers, came towards me and laid a hand on my arm.

'Good God, Lomont,' she said, 'you are quite pale. What happened to you yesterday evening? I sent you to fetch a dagger, but I did not mean you to leave, with or without it. What happened? Was it a migraine?' she said calmly, knowing that this explanation would satisfy everyone. (I did in fact have the misfortune – or perhaps the good fortune – sometimes to suffer the most painful neuralgia, which forced me to retire in the middle of a ball or to suffer like a martyr through dinner.)

'Lomont drinks too much,' said that rat d'Orty, having already availed himself too freely of the contents of his silver flask, from which he was woefully pouring the last few drops onto the ground. 'Lomont is a dangerous alcoholic.'

No one paid him any attention and his fatuous remark would have ended there had Gildas not added rather coldly: 'Is it true that you're a drunkard, Lomont? I've been told that you sometimes have visions – that you see things that don't exist.'

I was amazed to hear myself reply calmly and unconcernedly, almost languidly, 'I sometimes see things I shouldn't, yes. But it is a gift I alone have and no one shares – at least not in Angoulême.'

Gildas's sarcastic smile vanished and his eyes once more became those of a dog brought to heel, eyes dulled with unspeakable pain, the same eyes I had seen the day before, which were those of a blind man.

'I beg your pardon,' he said in a low voice.

And everyone was stilled for a moment by the tragic

tone of his voice, the voice of youth itself, that rang with candour, violence and despair.

'What's that you're saying?' asked d'Orty. 'You're talking in riddles, man. Can't you talk sense, for the love of God? Do you understand what they're saying, Countess?' he asked Flora, whose pensive eyes, imploring and fearful, flashed from her lover to me and back to her lover again.

My eyes met those so familiar to me, in which I generally encountered an expression of cruelty – the benevolent cruelty of friendship where there is no love – but which now were troubled, and now at last were raised to mine in supplication, without knowing what favour they craved; eyes which simply said, 'Not a word! Not a single word! I do not want to know.' I lowered my gaze beneath the new nakedness of her expression. At last it was the expression of a woman which she bestowed on me. I averted my eyes, ashamed for Gildas, ashamed for myself, ashamed for her. Without having to look, I saw her hand find his, and saw their fingers entwine in a convulsive embrace. I saw Gildas turn to face her, and when he held her close against his robust and faithless body that was infatuated with another woman, Flora entrusted herself to him without reserve.

Gildas's features were drawn, but he radiated a sombre happiness. My untimely interruption the previous day must have fired the imagination of that strumpet Martha, and every millimetre of Gildas's tanned body, every one of the hairs on his head, every muscle that flexed beneath his skin, every nerve, every atom of his manly body exuded a sense of satiety, of physical well-being, of the most complete, most animal-like satisfaction that no other man could fail to recognise. And this was the man my darling Flora loved, and to him that she was clinging; it was against his heart, which she could hear calmly beating, that she rested her head, without the least suspicion that there was a hand with dirty fingernails that could make it beat twice or three times as fast. I grabbed d'Orty's other hip-flask as it hung from his belt, almost tore it off him, and seared my throat with the foul liquor it contained, oblivious to what it was or how it tasted.

Gildas grew perceptibly paler and thinner. Flora spoke openly of her anxiety. Our company was amazed and attributed these symptoms to creative fervour. Parisian and Saintongean alike exclaimed over the demands of inspiration. In the end I too would surely have discerned a halo round the young man's head, had I not recently seen it between the legs of a maid servant.

Gildas, who had first of all, and not without a certain display of irritation, refused the alibi of his creative muse, now resigned himself to this convenient but farcical explanation. He did not speak to me, nor did I speak to him, but if anyone happened to allude in all innocence to a situation in any way resembling our own – or rather his – strangely enough it was I who blushed. We never referred to 'the afternoon in the gun-room', as I thought of it, but at least during the days that followed Gildas had the good grace not to disappear whenever I was present. And yet I was with them as often as the other guests – that is to say, all the time. Lunches, rides, hunts, fishing expeditions, balls, dinners, and suppers succeeded one another with a regularity unprecedented in Angoulême. Even Artemise herself found the pace exhausting and I noticed white hairs in her auburn tresses.

But advancing years seemed to have taken an even greater toll on her husband, Honoré Anthleme d'Aubec. I realised that he shared Gildas's obsession, though I really could not believe that this slut was able, unaided, to reduce to a state of exhaustion these two vigorous men, as well as the two louts she was also said to entertain.

Gildas and Honoré looked as if they were wasting away. They were becoming like skeletons, flayed by excruciating memories. And the woman who had brought them to this seemed not even to see them when her duties brought her into their presence. Her appearance in our midst would invariably prompt both Gildas and Honoré to make a conscious effort to avert their gaze, while in contrast the eyes of every other man in the room would converge on her. Gildas always turned to Flora – and looked on her ever more lovingly, I could not deny it – but the indifference of Honoré, our gallant prefect, became quite obvious and a cause of distress even to Artemise. In the end she perceived its meaning, and it came as a great shock much more to her pride than to her affections that her fool of a husband, cuckolded though he may have been for years without protest, was now actually deceiving her with a serving-girl. Had Honoré been enamoured of a lady drawn from the aristocracy, she might almost have derived some satisfaction from his passion. And equally, it was not his lying with a servant that offended Artemise, but the fact that he should continue to think of her when he was no longer in her arms was outrageous.

And he was thinking of her. He was obsessed with

her, ravaged by the thought of her. His full pink cheeks had become drawn and yellow. He drank heavily, became fretful about everything, and even lost interest in his financial affairs. So much so, that this man who used to do his accounts ten times a month no longer set foot in my office. And when I jokingly reproved him for his neglect, I was astounded by the vehemence of his reply: 'What do you expect me to do, my dear Lomont? Money is of no use to me at all.' And his voice was so harsh and strained that I closed the door to his office, and rushed to offer him an armchair, into which he collapsed and told me the whole story.

He had good reason to collapse. Whatever one might say, there are certain kinds of misery which can only be discreditable, unlike happiness which is always a cause for celebration. My passion for Flora had made me ridiculous, sad and humiliated, but at least I could console myself that neither my soul nor my conscience had suffered by it. There is no shame in vainly loving a woman worthy, as Flora was, of being loved. But that slut of a maid! Moreover, it seemed that quick as she might be to surrender to a suitor's desire, this was apparently a way of causing her lovers more pain than pleasure. Their passion, now inflamed by memory, grew intolerable. A vague desire for almost any woman was transformed into desire for one woman in particular: her. Especially when she refused even to look at them any more. Hardly had they been satisfied than she stole away from them, promising herself again, but never keeping her promises. She would not see them, then she would arrange to meet them in bizarre places, where she would come and give herself like a bitch in heat, or reject them without a word of explanation. Furthermore, and this surprised me, she would not take a penny from them, not a farthing from any of them – except perhaps from her two fine rustics who could ill afford the expense, and whom she milked for their few small coins whenever she joined her obscene fantasies to theirs.

These three vied with one another in their depravity, gave one another lessons in lewdness and sadism. I cannot describe the scenes that took place between them as Honoré, although he had once inadvertently chanced upon one of these performances, refused to tell me what he had seen. But I realised from what he said that although his attendance may have been inadvertent, by no means was it a chance encounter. The girl had deliberately arranged his discovery of them and had inflicted upon him the spectacle of her taking her pleasure with others, motivated not by voluptuousness with a capital V as Honoré would have it, but by what I called vice with a small v.

How could Gildas, who was able to call his own the most charming, the purest, the most lovely of women – a woman to whom he was obviously a lover beloved – how could he kneel before a slut already used by this gross prefect and two hirelings? I must have muttered my question aloud, for when Honoré heard it his complaints ceased and he looked at me suddenly with cold impatience. How can I describe it? The scene is before me still. In a building with closed shutters, I sat at the desk his predecessors had sat behind, beneath a picture of Louis-Philippe and the gaze of past prefects whose portraits hung on the walls around. It was a peaceful room, into which sunlight filtered through blinds. Honoré's subordinates could be heard working next door – the calm rise and fall of their voices and the rustling of paper. And he sat there struggling with his nightmare, once master of his own little world, now a frantic madman, just a few yards from his house, but a million miles from home. Our sole comforting reminder of the sunshine in the square outside were the parallel beams that passed through the blinds, gilding the powdery dust and resting on the parquet floors, occasionally reflecting from the buckle on Honoré's shoe, making it flash brightly and wink in the sun.

I was in sore need of those bright reflections. Shadows, dark and fearful, however ridiculous, filled my companion's story – a lurid story that I found all too convincing though it betrayed his hopeless naivety and foolishness. In response to my questions that were prompted by thoughts of Gildas, Honoré raised his head and repeated distractedly 'What? What?' His face was turned to me so that I saw his bloodshot eyes and the swollen lips he must have been chewing as he spoke – lips now drawn back in a spasm that seemed to convulse his face, making it hideously and incongruously suggestive, and horrible to look upon.

'Look here, Lomont,' he said in a grating and sibilant voice – his prefect's voice, the voice of a man of ambition. 'Look here, it's quite clear she's no ordinary whore. Don't you know, Lomont, d'Orty offered her a thousand francs to be his housekeeper, not just a maid. And Doillac wanted to give her his hunting lodge at Confolens, to set her up there with all the furniture. Do you know, she refused the money, the furniture, and the lodge? And do you know, her two brutish lovers had a fight to the death yesterday evening, with knives, and one of them is on his death-bed? And what's more, he's been asking for her and she won't go to him. Don't you understand? Men do whatever she asks of them. They will give her anything and everything, because she will take nothing. All of them, one after the other . . .'

'And I,' I said with a laugh, to stem this torrent of insanity, 'what have I ever offered her? What have I ever promised her or granted her?'

Honoré smiled. 'Your silence,' he said. 'Just your silence, and that is all she wants of you.'

I was suddenly infuriated, enraged by the realisation that he knew. 'I said nothing because of Flora, and only because of her,' I protested. 'I do not want Flora to be in any way involved in the affairs of maid servants and stableboys. The bestial couplings which you regard as your destiny are no concern of Flora's. And she will remain unsullied by them, of that I do assure you.'

I would have struck him then, but the storm broke before I landed the first blow. A sinister grumbling from the overcast sky erupted over the square, and a violent wind sweeping across the Place d'Armes suddenly banged shut thirty shutters all at once, and seemed to hurl itself at the paving stones. The sun suddenly went in, and I felt compelled to go and look through the window at the square outside. What I saw blown about the Place d'Armes, flying everywhere, were not only newspapers and the usual early fall of dead leaves but also an incredible wave of filth carried along by the wind from the suburbs – pieces of glass, corks, bits of discarded finery, the various unidentifiable rubbish from around the town cast out by its inhabitants. There was something deeply disturbing about this evidence of low life intruding on our bourgeois surroundings, this waste from another world, a world no more than two hundred yards distant. The people who lived round the square gazed, like myself, in amazement and indignation at these unspeakable objects. I stepped back and almost bumped into Honoré, who was looking over my shoulder.

'Now look here,' I said to Honoré, 'take a hold of yourself. After all, there aren't a million ways of making love to a girl. According to the Hindus, there are only thirty-six, which is many more than I know of. But pleasure is always pleasure, old chap, nothing more nor less.'

There was a moment's silence before Honoré replied in a low voice: 'A great deal more and a great deal less, Lomont, I swear to you.'

And this quiet, almost naked voice made a deeper impression on me than all his previous impassioned confessions. He said no more, he made no further complaint, even his suffering seemed to have ceased, and yet, in that stormy late afternoon, in that atmosphere so bizarre I could smell the lilac from across the square, for a moment Honoré seemed to me like a man condemned to death – a man already dead.

'I am going to ask Flora to dismiss her,' I murmured in despair.

It was obviously the only chance Honoré would ever get to buy this hussy lodged at Margelasse. But even more than my egotism and my melancholy, I felt a sense of urgency, of danger, a sudden sense of imminent catastrophe that dwarfed all my own hopes.

Honoré looked up at me with the plaintive eyes of a sick animal, and said to me quite simply, 'If she goes, I shall follow her, Lomont. Can you understand that?'

And his hopeless resignation broke my heart.

When I arrived back at Nersac, I rushed straight to the kitchen, but neither the Anjou wine nor the cheese I devoured were in the least heartening.

D'Orty's CHÂTEAU WAS SOME DISTANCE from Angoulême so that when he held a grand ball there, everyone was obliged to spend the night, and each guest was to travel with his or her valet or maid, who would help them dress for the ball. I decided to take advantage of these circumstances to tackle the troublesome wench. I would make it clear to her that she was to leave, without giving Flora notice and without explaining the reason for her departure. I decided to take enough money with me to exact her compliance. For her refusal of Honoré's bribes meant nothing to me except that she must want to see the colour of our money. There was no other explanation for her conduct since she loved no man. I might have thought her susceptible to Gildas's good looks if, in the course of his confession, Honoré had not admitted to having had her himself just the day before, in a stable box. There was no doubt she was a woman whose body knew no restraint, a perversion of nature, and the smile she had proffered me over Gildas's shoulder when I had surprised them – that mocking provocative smile and the devilish expression in her almond-shaped eyes – were proof to me that, since this trollop cared for no one, she must therefore have regard for money. I was acquainted with this kind of deviousness, my duties as a notary having afforded me an insight into the cupidity and wiles of women. In short, I was resolved to be firm but generous, and if the sum of one thousand crowns might free my friends and fellow men from their dementia, the money was but a small sacrifice compared with the sacrifice of my own hopes of winning Flora.

So, after I had finished work, I set out for Cognac. Since I was travelling in Honoré's carriage, I was unable to avoid being subjected to further confidences as we journeyed. However, I gave the poor man no encouragement.

'I loathe her,' he said, his wild eyes staring through the window as though we were travelling through uncharted territory. 'I hate her and yet only with her is life bearable.'

He was like a man who borrows money and realises too late that his debt is ruinous, and there is no escape. In his case, the body he had acquired on credit – for which he had mortgaged his life, his reputation and his career – had been immediately reclaimed. As for the exorbitant interest, that was his suffering and his obsession. For his desire was no longer an uncertain, unspecified desire for an unknown woman; it had been replaced by the demands of particular images, gestures and memories. The vagueness of his desires had given way to a huge blinding sun, towards which he advanced, eyes wide open, reeling on the edge of a recollection dreadful in its exactitude. It is common knowledge that in music, as in culinary matters, it is not discovery which is the overwhelming experience but rediscovery. The greatest pleasure lies not in encountering a new sensation but in the recognition of similarities and differences. Honoré and Gildas must have had lacerating memories judging by their incredulous martyred expressions. For martyrs they both were. At her request, or rather her insistence, the two of them had written love-letters to this hussy, and she had read and re-read them until she could remember them well enough to torment her lovers by quoting passages from them. She would recite snatches at whim, whenever they met, rendering grotesque and obscene in the cold light of day words written in the exhausted fever of the night, words all too deeply and too keenly felt, written in ink that was already fading in the sun, or on the contrary was indecently burnished by it. Moreover, she would make mistakes, or pretend to, and would quote to one words that the other had written – the most intimate phrases, of course – laughing heartily when the poor wretch, in fury or despair, or in a hopeless attempt to assert his dignity, would point out her error and would advise her that she was mistaken as to the identity of the author. That would bring tears of laughter to her eyes.

'What of it?' she would say. 'Since it's the same person who receives them . . .'

Honoré she had designated 'Monsieur, the prefect of mushrooms', since he had returned shamefaced and agitated from a painful rendezvous deep in a wood, and now she had him eating out of her hand, prepared to do anything, resigned to everything except to living without her. But this total surrender was a source of annoyance to Martha. He no longer seemed to suffer when she taunted him with phrases that two times out of three he had not written – for d'Orty also wrote to her – phrases, moreover, which seemed no more ridiculous to him than his own. It seemed that there was only Gildas left to conquer – Gildas, who still refused to denounce Flora in Martha's presence and who therefore offered greater opportunity for cruelty, and at the same time, as she told Honoré, was most adept at pleasuring her. She taunted Honoré with praise of Gildas's handsomeness, drawing comparisons with Honoré's own lack of distinction in this respect. And yet I felt that of all those gentlemen whose love – as well as their person and, until now, their property – she so disdainfully scorned, Gildas was the only one who might have been capable of winning her affections. But if she loved Gildas, why did she not run away with him? Gildas was now a rich man; his plays and books were everywhere on sale. And if she did not love him, why offer herself to him, making love with a frenzy that poor Honoré so relished in describing?

I speak of Martha without having properly introduced her, but that is essential if one is to understand exactly what kind of woman she was, and to make sense of this story.

But who is it that I am suddenly anxious not to mislead? It must be time for me to stop. But – and may the gods of literature forgive me – I now enjoy the hour I spend every day hunched over my notebook. I often forget the time while I am writing. The other evening my housekeeper grew very concerned, supper-time having long since passed, and fearing I might be unwell, she called to me from the stairs. She was deeply reassured in this regard because I dined in very good spirits, thanks to every scribbler's sense of exuberance, surrounded as I was at table by Flora, Honoré, d'Orty and Martha, whom I had restored to life, or so it seemed. I drank a silent but merry toast to Honoré, to my deceased friends, to my absent enemy, and to my beautiful love, distraught and lost for ever.

THE CHÂTEAU IN COGNAC THAT d'Orty had inherited was one of the finest in the country. Of immense proportions, its fine structure lent to rooms uncluttered by furniture a sense of spaciousness which I delighted in contemplating. This sense of space was not in evidence on the night of the ball. D'Orty had invited the whole province, no doubt in order to dazzle his servant-mistress, and had expended all at once the money she had scorned to take. The guests were royally received. The mansion blazed with a thousand candles, a thousand fires, a thousand flowers. Two sumptuous buffet tables had been laid in two large rooms, and there were fifty footmen from Bordeaux and Périgueux in attendance all dressed in d'Orty's livery.

Everyone was masked and we were all anxious not to be too soon identified. Each man and each woman for this reason wore a new outfit for the occasion and, in accordance with the wishes of the master of the house, masks were to be removed by two o'clock at the latest, but not before midnight.

Poor d'Orty! His intelligence seemed to have ceded

territory to attacks of despair. I recognised him at once by his reedy voice, but I pretended not to know him. I also instantly recognised Flora, dressed in midnight blue, the blue of her eyes which readily betrayed her identity to a discerning interested party. Nevertheless, I greeted her with an air of confusion as 'Madame', which made her laugh, softly at first, but then quite heartily. Her laugh was so infectious we were obliged to remove our masks after five minutes and reveal ourselves in order to dry our childish tears.

'My make-up must look terrible,' she said wiping her eyes. 'But honest to goodness, Lomont, would you really say to a woman you did not know "Good-day Madame, my compliments, Madame" in that tone of voice? You sounded like a comic villain . . . Admit that you recognised me straight away . . .'

I energetically denied it, and we went and danced in the ballroom. There we were much applauded so well did we keep time with the music. After three waltzes and a polka, Flora pleaded for mercy. I left her sitting in a tiny armchair and set out at her request to look for Gildas, whom she had twice seen smiling at her when we began to dance, but not since then. Like everyone else, he was in costume and his mask was gold and glittering, she told me so that I should recognise him. Twice I conscientiously traversed the crowd of people – of whom there were as many from Paris, Lyon and Bordeaux as from Angoulême – looking for the golden mask, but without success, and I cannot say I was surprised. It was, therefore, only after spending ten minutes searching downstairs that I finally made my way to the rooms that had been allotted to Flora and Gildas, and where I had earlier that evening taken a glass of port with them. Along empty corridors, past empty bedrooms, through empty cloakrooms, I passed from one dark room to another, listening to the silence, continuing towards other identical rooms.

The last one I tried was the one for which I had been looking. In the darkness, the silence was disturbed by the sound of rustling silk, of sheets being thrown aside, and a sound I instantly recognised: that of one body beating against another, faster and faster, transfixing me on the threshold. I closed the door and leaned my head against the wall of the corridor, covering my ears when I heard the woman's orgasmic cry rise like that of a deer in a paroxysm of rage and suffering and violence, and then break insufferably on a deep note of unbearable animality. It drew me back into the room with the sole intention of tearing Gildas away from that woman, to usurp his place and force myself between those legs and into the body from which that voice had issued, the carnal cry of the female that I had immediately identified, the cry that is all men's due, but to which they so rarely lay claim. I threw myself at the door, but the panel was locked on that side, and I stunned myself, so that all at once, as I regained my senses, I felt as if I had just awoken. The silence was deadly, uneasy, and almost more intolerable than the cry uttered minutes before by that inhuman voice, terrible in its sensuality and naturalness.

I do not know how I found my way to the staircase nor by what miracle I recognised in a mirror the haggard stranger who descended the stairs as myself, Nicholas Lomont, my face distorted as I have seen people disfigured by a great fright. And for a moment I panicked at the thought of going back to the crowd below. Someone bumped into me, and as he turned to apologise I saw his mask and realised this might be a way out of my difficulty. I remembered having put mine in my pocket as I went upstairs half an hour earlier. I spent five minutes looking for it before a footman passed by and noticed the swelling and bruises on my forehead. He applied ice and cold compresses to my injuries, and went to obtain another mask from his master. I sat waiting in the kitchen, surrounded by servants who here looked as busy, as austere and exhausted as they had seemed calm and smiling in the drawing-room. My presence did not disturb them at all, and because they seemed not to see me, I formed the impression I had been waiting a long time. At last my neglectful footman returned, out of breath, and he gave me a new mask and a kind of turban that would disguise the cuts and bruises on my head. I tipped him a few coins, and this wondrous nurse insisted I drink a potion that would, he said, put an honest man back on his feet again. And indeed I was quite happy now to rejoin the throng, rehearsing some stammering excuse that I might give Flora for not having found her lover.

Then I saw him standing near her, talking to her with animation, gaiety, and warmth. Flora was responding to him in all tenderness, with a smile in the depths of her eyes that hid nothing from him. He looked so happy, so passionate, and so sincere that the women who danced by ceased to pay attention to their partners. I could see them trying to find fault with Flora so that his happiness should be less cruel to witness. For there was happiness there as well as love: an infinite replete love, a love that was absolute; and happiness of which everyone dreams and which everyone seeks, the happiness that illuminated those two faces and which depended on the whim of a chambermaid. Gildas was completely satisfied in his sexuality, in his pride and in his sincerity, and he came to make an offering of his happiness to the woman he truly loved, the woman he cherished and esteemed beyond all things, the woman he had deceived only minutes before for the sole purpose, perhaps, of being able to love her better afterwards. Gildas was so handsome, above all so young, and his coupling with another woman was so innocently enjoyed that I began to understand those hedonists who argue a great distinction between body and soul, a disparity that was never meant to be reconciled. As if pleasure were innocent in men; as if the skin in all its pores, the senses in their exultant weariness, the nerves in their happy exhaustion – as if everything which gives us pleasure, restores us also to an original innocence. As if it were true that a contract whereby pleasure is shared, given and received – an exchange of certain like actions, of a like thirst, and a like fever – is in itself acceptable. Gildas Caussinade's body, the body of this almost improperly handsome and gifted nobody to whom too much happened, was to my exasperated and jealous eyes quite innocent. The only guilty party, which betrayed itself, forgot itself and hated itself for doing so, was Gildas's soul, and it was his soul to which Flora's faithful body responded; a soul which, like a crippled old maid, lurched down endless corridors in pursuit of her infamous and delicious prey, the agile, spirited and hungry body of Gildas.

As a witness to all this, I am obliged to confess that rather than fury or jealousy or scorn, it was envy that he inspired in me. But what envy! Not envy for the life he led and would continue to lead with Flora, but envy for the fifteen minutes he had just enjoyed. There was now a greater despair and a greater bitterness in my heart, as though it were easier to allow a rival to enjoy happiness than passion. For happiness binds him hand and foot to his companion to the grave, bequeathing to us survivors misery of course, but also passion, its vagaries and its freedom from restraint. I realised that I would have given my left arm to hear once more that tortured cry of gratification of only a short while ago, and my right arm if she had uttered it while lying beneath me. In short, I realised that I was drunk, and that the footman was to blame, and that I ought to escape this ballroom and sweat out my intoxication elsewhere. Once more I made my way along those corridors, heading towards that dangerous woman to fulfil my mission as a virtuous man and a loyal friend.

I FOUND HER SITTING IN a low chair at the foot of the bed in which she had so recently voiced her cries. Now she was perfectly groomed, the very picture of decorous good manners. She looked like the nun who sits at the convent gate, her black blouse neatly tucked into a skirt of small-checked material that almost covered her nun's shoes. She was sewing, or appeared to be sewing, a dress that sparkled black and gold, which I had never seen Flora wear. I stopped in the doorway, and coughed. She glanced up at me in annoyance and then surprise when, by swaying slightly as I entered the room, I betrayed my state of inebriation. But her disdain, if such it was, did not affect me. I no longer saw that austere face, that inscrutable, almost insolent face which set her apart and made her so unlike the rest of Flora's deferential staff. What I saw was a skin so delicate and white, a skin so pale that it would be instantly marked by the red flush of anger. I gazed at her down-turned mouth, as greedy as it was scornful, at her cheeks set wide apart, at the sweep of her iron-grey eyes. I examined this woman's face feature by feature and I had no difficulty in recreating the face from which that howl of love had issued only a short time ago. She must have seen something in my eyes which arrested her hand, needle poised, her eyes riveted to mine; eyes that were interested, curious, amused, perhaps, in which I could see no trace of shame or fear, not even of embarrassment. Rather artfully, I was counting on gaining some advantage from the discomfiture of my adversary. For what woman would not suffer some discomfort in the presence of a man who a few minutes earlier had discovered her in the act of fornication? But why do I ask this ridiculous question since I already know the answer. What woman would do this? Only one: this one. I ought to have written: I had come face to face with the only woman I know who could remain unabashed . . . and so on.

I am indulging in the literary affectations I so much abhorred in the past. And as I begin to appreciate what spurious problems and disingenuous questions, what stratagems are exploited in literature to arouse the interest of a perhaps somnolent reader, my head spins at the thought of all the other ploys to which we resort, no doubt unconsciously, in everyday life to kindle some interest in the fortunes of a character who is important in a different way, but also more difficult to please, alas, than any reader – our selves.

'I have something to say to you,' I said at last, taking great pains to speak clearly, an effort which liberated in me an unaccustomed talkativeness that had never previously been stimulated by alcohol.

So I treated her to a fine speech that was by turn solemn, hypocritical, threatening and insinuating, rambling and angry. I spoke to her of Flora, of Flora's goodness and high regard for her. I told Martha that not even Paris could satisfy her insatiable lust for lovers, but that the police would remove her there by force if necessary, if she did not take the ten thousand crowns that I was offering her, and consider herself dismissed. How had I come to multiply the thousand crowns I had decided on the day before to ten thousand? I did not understand it myself, and the only explanation I could think of was the footman's tonic; his damned concoction must have prompted this ruinous liberality.

All in all, I was pompous, emotional and ridiculous, and certainly very long-winded. The sound of music from the ballroom could be heard indistinctly in this room, so peaceful in the half-darkness, where I sat opposite a mere housemaid, who listened to me without taking her eyes off me for a moment, with a dreamy, tranquil but totally attentive expression on her face. After a moment, in the full flow of my arguments, I stood up and paced the room, while her eyes followed me, staring with a limpid steely gaze at my shoulders, my knees, my chest, my hair, looking me over from head to toe, again and again, like a horse dealer.

I did not immediately find her scrutiny offensive – the kind of scrutiny it is usually the privilege of men to enjoy with regard to women – because her looks of appraisal were above all quite candid, certainly more candid then lewd, despite their shamelessness. But when I realised what her expression signified, I stopped dead in my tracks just three yards in front of her, and tried to hide my confusion by continuing to stammer out a few words to which she did not listen. There was a ghost of a smile on her lips as her eyes came to rest somewhere about the level of my groin. An expression of approval on her face made me examine myself and on discovering the reason for her smile, I blushed scarlet with rage and embarrassment. She glanced up at me and put her sewing on the table. She rose, still holding my gaze, and it was with a kind of holy terror that I saw her walk towards me and, with a light imperious touch that I could feel through my clothes, she placed her hand on the cause of my shame and her amusement. I barely heard her murmur, 'But of course . . . in a little while?' Then she left the room singing softly to herself.

Her exit left me nonplussed in my absurdity, and quite unmanned. What on earth was I doing reacting like a virgin at his first sight of a woman? Obviously my high-handed discourse and my worthy advice – and I mean advice, because after all, it was not my place to be giving her orders – were robbed of all credibility, if indeed they ever had any. My virtuous stance had been completely undermined by my being as hopelessly susceptible to Martha as any other man. I was now ready to believe in Martha's power since I myself had been unable to remain impervious to her physical magnetism. And yet I had so effortlessly and so sincerely despised her moral character, she inspired in me such distaste, that it seemed to me that my body had erred, and that the warm and comfortable flesh which, with a few bones and a few clever feats of engineering, enveloped my soul, had not been able to differentiate between Flora and this harlot. I was greatly disillusioned in myself. All my life I had stupidly laughed at stories of people who were slaves to their senses. My body had always obeyed me, and obeyed me still, promptly and faithfully. Since birth I had only been made conscious of its existence, apart from the pleasure it afforded me, by some very minor demands, which have remained the same for the past thirty years. These demands consisted of telling me I should lie down and keep warm when I had a fever, and that after a restless night I should not drink wine the following day. As for my body's sexual appetite, this necessitated a trip to Bordeaux from time to time, to a house where I could surrender this all too corporeal but prudish carcass to the ministrations of a nurse with a red lantern. It was a three-hour ride to this house where I arrived dusty but happy, and as impatient to lie down against the warmth of another human body as to relieve this body of its pent-up desires. My body was a good servant to me, but sometimes it reacted badly to solitude; then I would offer it in the shape of a whore the warmth, the gestures, the scent and gentleness of a woman; a life shared with another person, if only for an hour. And each time this would leave my body spent and myself melancholy, my appetite dulled and my body hungry for more. And those girls of the night seemed to know this, perhaps they guessed, since they would suddenly become very maternal and gentle, like all women to whom we have given pleasure, or rather all women who allow us to believe we have. A body that lay beside mine for a price, a body that had been bribed, whether or not against its wishes, was the only body against which I could extend my own when, overcome with loneliness and deprived of tenderness, my own body – a human animal of no interest to anyone, and still less to Flora – began to protest and grow restive despite my sternest moral disapproval.

I awoke as if from a dream and realised with amazement that only half an hour had passed since I had launched into my speech, although it seemed I had been in this room for at least three hours. My well-turned phrases, that had been sufficiently inspired to enable me to forget their total ineffectualness, had made me feel quite light-headed. It was their subtlety that had escaped this wench: it had all gone over her head. And attempting to delude myself in this way, and thereby lessen the shame of having been routed, I returned to the rooms below, descending the staircase I had so recently climbed confident of my success.

It was not yet midnight. I was surrounded by masked faces and found myself not far from Flora and Gildas, who stood side by side, encircled by a crowd of people. I could hear him chattering gaily, much more gaily than Flora, it seemed to me as I watched them. A new bitterness compressed her lips. I broke through the group gathered around her and asked her to dance. For some reason she seemed relieved to accept. Usually she did not like to be too far from Gildas. From the moment he was in the same room, she was instinctively drawn to him, but equally apparent was a need to preserve some distance between them, which generally prevented her from so much as brushing against her lover's body, or even laying a finger on him. It has just occurred to me that lovers truly in love, especially those who have given each other proof of their love just before leaving the privacy of the bedroom, if they chance to come close in public, take a step backwards, and retreat as if contact with each other would badly burn their flesh. If their overwhelming desire is a guilty secret, especially if this is the case, these happy lovers are then so pale, so anxious to avoid contact with each other that, despite themselves, they reveal their forbidden intimacy – an intimacy consummated in an afternoon of frantic and exhausting passion, after which they are all at once sceptical, full of wonder at what it was that threw them into such confusion and brought them so much happiness. These are moments when lovers – men especially – are aware of being single, and are quite happy with their unmarried status, and wish to remain so, their bodies selfish in their satisfaction, which allows these bachelors to take a cynical pride in their cold detachment. And yet they will in a flash remember, at a chance inflection of the voice, a gesture of the hand, or something said, all the sweetness of that afternoon of love, all the brevity of those few short hours, all the exquisite abandonment of passion.

I shall bring to a conclusion this long and pointless homily. In fact I am quite happy to stop, with no feelings of regret for denying future generations further reflections of this nature. That said, let us return to poor d'Orty's parquet floors across which I was waltzing with Flora.

WE WERE DANCING ONCE MORE, but this time I made no attempt to take advantage of Flora's surrender to the music and of my leading her to hold her tightly in my arms. For Flora was suddenly sad. She had foregone all resistance, her body bent back from the waist in sympathy with the movement of the waltz; but her leaning back was not giddy self-abandon, just as her pliability was not a general limpness. How can I describe it? She was not cowed; unlike other human beings who, when they sense the imminence of disaster or misfortune, bow their heads to their chests and present their less vulnerable backs as a surface for the blows and injuries of existence, she was not stooped in submission. Flora threw back her shoulders, exposing her neck. She seemed to have decided that misfortune would strike her only head on, and already she was turning her face to right and left in time with the music in what looked like a long slow denial of her future, though she knew not what it was. Her face in profile, her half-closed eyes, the corner of her mouth, the paleness of her cheek – pale rather than white – beneath eloquent blue-grey eyes . . . all this beauty would soon be of no use to her, and would even become hateful to her. We danced, we waltzed, we whispered, we laughed. She continued to turn her head to the same rhythm and, each time, her mass of silky golden hair seemed to intervene between Flora and her life, or rather, seemed to try and hide her from her destiny.

It was then that I was overwhelmed by the most powerful upsurge of feeling I have ever known, an experience of the utmost intensity, and certainly unique in uniting in a single plea to a God in whom I did not believe, my intelligence, my body and my heart; also my moral conscience, my pride, my courage and my vulnerability. A burning wave swept over me, so completely, with such forcefulness and at the same time such tenderness that I realised then, in the gentleness of it, that she would never return to me, that never again would I thrill to this swell of emotion, this perfect harmony, this strange power. How many of us were there that evening, among the two hundred to three hundred people dancing, who had enjoyed that privilege? For I was one of a privileged few; whatever happened to me afterwards, I was privileged to have been thus immersed in the fullness of that flood, and to have drowned in it. Previously I had dared to attribute to mere imitations, to pathetic bubbles of feeling the name of that rush of emotion; a name that was for myself and for every human being, from birth until death, the greatest of hungers and the least satisfied: tenderness. Suddenly I loved Flora as I had never loved anyone, because I no longer wanted her for myself. I no longer wanted her to love me passionately, nor to be jealous of me, nor even to live with me. I no longer wanted her as I had wanted her every second of my life for nearly two years. Suddenly I was no longer Lomont who wanted Flora de Margelasse, I was just someone who wanted another person to be happy, and nothing more. I wanted Flora to be happy – with Gildas, with anyone.

Her face was open, gentle and vulnerable; it was the face of a thirty-year-old woman whose past had been cruel. She had courage, gaiety and a kind heart. A woman of rather impulsive enthusiasms, she loved poetry, and her eyes were so unhappy sometimes at the sight of my unhappiness because of her. She behaved with impeccable good manners, and yet was sincere. She was uncompromising in her sentiments but friendly towards others. This child grown to womanhood wrote verses in secret, verses which, although lyrical, were weakened by the extremity of their sadness and languor. She so innocently wanted to be happy, needed to be happy, and had reason to be so, she so wanted to love as much as to be loved, so wanted to give as well as to receive. She was no more capable of wickedness than she was of meanness or mistrust, and she had staked everything, all that she owned, all that was to come, her fears, her past, her present, her future, her honour, her whole life, on a peasant-poet younger than she, a man who was still a child. She had loved him in silence and then refused to humiliate him by remaining silent, as soon as she knew that her love was reciprocated. And when I beheld this tender-hearted woman who would undoubtedly and inescapably suffer most horribly, from a distance I took her to my heart, dried all the tears she was to shed on my shoulder, calmed her sobbing, and comforted her in her sadness with the purest and most selfless devotion. In short, I gave her my life, my blood, and all the long hours of my life to come. I made her a gift of myself at the very moment I abandoned the desire that she should be mine.

I saw Flora through a kind of phosphorescent veil,

and while I could still see the other dancers, they appeared in an artistic nebulousness which I could not explain as normally my vision was excellent. Neither could I explain the vicelike grip which I felt around my neck, nor the weakness at my knees, and I stumbled, missed a beat, two beats, confusing some dancers whose outline was more than blurred; they were completely drained of colour, by what phenomenon I knew not. It was Flora who gave me the key to this unease, to my giddiness, when, shaken out of her reverie by my drunken lurching, she raised her eyes, and stopped dead in the middle of the waltz, right there in the centre of the room, and earnestly entreated me in a very low shocked voice, 'Nicholas, what's the matter? You are weeping.' It was only then that I understood the cause of the semi-blindness that had overcome me, and the hand with which I automatically touched my cheek simply confirmed what I then already knew. I was stunned. There was I, thirty years of age, a big strong man, rooted to the spot with hot tears springing from my eyes, springing from some moment in my life I could not identify, unaware at the time that it was my future I was already lamenting – mine and that of my friends, my fine, gay, charming friends, whose only concern that evening seemed to be the dancing.

Flora took me by the hand as if I were a child and led me between the dancers without incurring too much damage; there was just the little red-haired fellow who kicked me and did not even apologise. I would have seized him by the collar if my eyes had not been swimming in tears and if I had not needed to blow my nose – I would do better to look less ridiculous before I attempted to sow terror and contrition in the heart of an unknown red-head. Outside was a bench where Flora made me sit down, dried my eyes, held my hand and looked at me with such sadness and tenderness that my tearful cold, as I insisted on calling it, redoubled in intensity and I had to clench my jaws most cruelly. But I could still feel gushing pitilessly out of me the round hot droplets that were eager to emerge, having accumulated behind my eyelids since my earliest youth, since the last time I cried, a good twenty years ago, it seemed. In their hurry to escape the prison of my insensitivity and well-mannered bourgeois restraint, my tears stung me as they poured forth, burning my eyelashes. Because of Flora, I forced myself to smile, one of those bewildered unconvincing smiles with which one greets unhappiness that defies explanation, even when it is one's own unhappiness.

'What is the matter?' Flora asked. 'What is wrong with you, Nicholas? I am your friend, and the thought of your unhappiness breaks my heart.'

'It's nerves,' I said tentatively. 'That must surely be the trouble.'

But I was cut short by a suddenly authoritative Flora.

'Your nerves? What nerves? Come, come, you don't suffer from nerves. I beg you, do not lie to me. You need say nothing, if you prefer, but do not feel obliged to give me such wretched excuses. Your nerves . . . your nerves . . .' She continued raising to heaven eyes filled with amusement. 'Nicholas Lomont talks to me of his nerves, and at the same time weeps uncontrollably! But it's enough to make one lose faith in God! Nicholas, listen to me. You and Gildas are the two people I love most in the world. If you cannot tell me the reason for your tears, at least you should know that they distress me greatly, and that all that I have is yours, and that you are very dear to me.'

And she suddenly stood up, leaned towards me and kissed me gently on my eyelids, my cheeks, my forehead, my nose; and brushing her lips against mine, she murmured, 'Your face is in a terrible state, Mr Lomont.

You have made me thirsty, and I am going to find you something to drink. Don't cry any more hunched over like that, it's more than I can bear to see you that way. Stand up at least and cry over the lawn . . .'

As I let her go, I was at last smiling with happiness and love and affection. I was smiling at my good fortune, for it was my good fortune that this woman should love me a little, and that she should have treated me as she would a child called Nicholas, the Nicholas I continued to be and who had not yet grown up, but whom she knew to be more important than Nicholas the lawyer.

She returned with a glass of Bouzy which I drained in a single draft, like a man, like the man Nicholas had become once more, and who, despite his reddened eyes, his naturally large nose swollen with tears, seemed nonetheless to attract this angelic woman's affection since, with kindness and gentleness, she covered my face with the black mask she had brought me – my third that evening.

I had lost the first in some deserted corridor, the second in the large drawing-room, but I hoped the third would be the last one I needed. I hoped that circumstances would not call for half a dozen. It was barely one o'clock. I had arrived at d'Orty's at ten. I had danced ten waltzes; twice I had wandered along empty corridors; I had come upon the cry of a woman making love; I had lectured that same slut on her morals; I had been flooded with tenderness and awash with tears; all this in the space of three hours, three masks, three Lomonts. I thought the most sensible thing would be to take this third person to bed and exchange the mask for a cotton night-cap which I did not possess; but I experienced a confused longing for one, in place of this black bandeau, just as I would have liked to exchange my violent feelings for a peaceful sleep. I was on my way out, but too late! Fate had already intervened; destiny had taken its place in the dance. To my appalled eyes it presented the disastrous aspect of a blighted love affair that had until then been a happy one – at least for one of the two lovers, for Gildas must have realised that it could only end in frightful misery. Gildas, even when he laughed, must have felt his teeth chattering in terror at the thought of his sin, of that outrage so seductive that even now I half-envy him.

Flora walked towards him, and while I continued to gaze at Gildas's handsome tanned face, it was suddenly distorted by an indescribable fury which made me hasten my steps to reach him and the object of his rage before Flora. It was the red-head who had bumped into me shortly before, and whose name was Choiseux. He was a marquis and also Duke of Chantasse, the most arrogant nobleman in all Saintonge, the most obsessed with his rank and the observance due him.

'Your arrival is timely,' he said turning to Flora, his pinched face glowing with a malevolent joy. 'Very timely, cousin – you do remember that we are cousins?'

'Yes,' said Flora, her voice full of anxious surprise. 'Yes, I know. Your great-uncle and my grandfather . . . But what is the meaning of all this? Why are you so pale, Gildas?' she asked her lover, not listening to the forceful reply of her red-haired cousin, which took the form of a huntsman's whistling that would call the dogs to heel, and coming as it did in an interval of silence in the violin-playing, transfixed the whole assembly. It was a coarse, vulgar gesture which, given the presence of ladies, not even the King of France himself should have allowed himself.

'I was saying to this peasant who thinks himself a lord,' said Henry de Choiseux, 'that he did not belong here among people of quality and that if I were him I should leave. I went so far as to say, cousin, that I knew you consorted with a poet, but I had not realised that this poet looked after rabbits, harvested the crops on my cousins' land, and fed their pigs. I find this monstrous in one who would have us believe he has won the heart of a lady to whom I am related by blood.'

'Choiseux, you are mad,' said d'Orty, who had rushed to the scene, and seemed determined quite rightly to assert his authority as master of the house. 'Choiseux, I insist that you retract those words or leave my house. Gildas is my guest.'

There was a silence, during which those present drew cautiously closer, and it was as if the two men were being locked into a vice which would prevent their reconciliation.

'He can stay in this room,' said Choiseux, his mouth hardened with bitterness and his pock-marked face hideous with anger. 'But in that case, let him carry trays or sweep the floor. I will not have him dancing before my eyes with any of the ladies present, whose fathers perhaps died at the hands of his relatives. Your memory is short, d'Orty. You must be mad to invite labourers into your house after what they did to our forefathers.'

Gildas, who had turned white, then red, then white again, stepped forward with a lifeless smile on his face and said in a clear voice: 'I have harvested crops, it is true, Sir Good-for-Nothing, and it would give me great pleasure to thrash you with a scythe, a sword, or what you will. You have only to give the word.'

'I only cross swords with men of my own standing,' Choiseux began, but Gildas landed him such a heavy blow that he staggered backwards.

His brother – called ironically 'Little' Choiseux because, at twenty, he was so well built and corpulent, and as dull-witted as his brother was sharp – threw himself at Gildas. For a moment there were three ruffians brawling in front of the ladies, then four when I aimed a hefty kick at the brother of the man who had insulted Gildas. One woman screamed shrilly and fainted, or feigned to do so, and without having to look round I knew it was Artemise. The effect of this was to calm everyone; to be more accurate, it put everyone in a great state of agitation, but forced them out of their bemusement.

D'Orty went from one to another, from me to Norbert de Choiseux, from Gildas to Henry the marquis, and in five minutes it was decided that we would duel the following day at dawn, with swords or pistols; the insult being adjudged to be mutual, the choice of weapons was left to our adversaries. I make no secret of the fact that I was terrified at the time, never having drawn a sword except against the rats in my attic, and being no more adept at wielding a pistol than I was at manipulating a fan. The violins started playing again, and everyone took to the floor, laughing too loudly or whispering. I thought the evening was over then, and I awaited the morning that would see the end of my life.

IN THE MEANTIME D'ORTY HAD been proved right; his ball was the finest of the season, indeed of the century, and it would be the one people would continue to talk about in great detail even in Paris. It was just after half past one. I added the duel to the outrageous list of my activities that evening, and danced with Artemise, who was at fever-pitch with excitement and clung to my body, my poor endangered body, with a passionate intensity to which I would have happily succumbed ten years earlier but which now left me cold.

Henry de Choiseux divided his time between Paris and Cognac, where his estate lay, meeting rebuffs from celebrated Parisiennes that were transformed by his accounts into conquests when he returned to the province. What is more, he was not only irascible but afflicted by an illness which allowed only short respite to the nerves and the mental stability of its victims. Having fulfilled what he considered to be his duty, and considering himself the hero of the evening as well as the champion of the aristocracy, Henry de

Choiseux made every effort to be droll and light-hearted for the following hour. His grating laugh and loud voice could be heard in every corner of d'Orty's ballroom, large as it was, so much so that when they were heard no more I grew alarmed. Yes indeed, I was strangely anxious when I could no longer hear that stupid self-important animal, that mindless ass, whose foolish victim I was to become, braying inanities. Just a poor country lawyer, I was no more blue-blooded than I was able to prevent my blood from running cold at the prospect of my demise.

Then I noticed Choiseux take the floor with a partner I did not recognise. There were still perhaps twenty people who had not yet dared remove their masks, and Choiseux was dancing with one of these – a woman in a black-and-gold gown, whom I had not seen that evening, and who danced extremely well, or so it seemed to me from the veiled depths of my sombre thoughts. Gildas and Flora were standing some distance away, talking very quietly and very feverishly to each other. Flora was drained of colour, even her lips were bloodless, and she was gazing at Gildas, scouring his face, his features, his body, his hands, with all the avidness of a mistress whose lover is to be stolen from her by the sword or pistol. But I knew Gildas had become a very good swordsman and a fine shot after two years of lessons in Paris, and I must confess I therefore feared only for my own life. But with the exception of Flora and perhaps Artemise, grown amorous ten years too late, I was alone in my fears.

Henry de Choiseux seemed fascinated by his dancing partner. He was not the only one, because as soon as the polka he was dancing came to an end, I saw three men converge on her, practically knocking one another over and not stopping to apologise. One of them was d'Orty. Having been the first to remove his mask – as befitted the master of the house – and expose his red cheeks and his air of stupidity, he was now pale and serious, and looked almost haunted. The second suitor for the next dance with the mysterious woman was our prefect, Honoré d'Aubec himself, who had seemed strained all evening, and whose face remained masked, perhaps to conceal its madness. And the third man who had just dashed the length of the room and reached her at the same time as d'Orty was none other than Gildas. The unknown lady looked splendid. Her black hair, which was almost concealed beneath a magnificent array of jewels; that sublimely airy dress whose jet brilliance was somehow disturbing; the full and sulking mouth that showed beneath her mask; the carriage of her head; her hands; the smallness of her waist, and its strength that could be detected beneath the tulle and satin; the deep throaty laugh; and the sparkle of her eyes behind the mask – all this conspired to fascinate an ordinary man, but terrified me. For the moment she looked in my direction, I knew it was Martha. It was she towards whom I was involuntarily drawn and to whom d'Orty introduced me as his excellent friend Nicholas Lomont. He calmly referred to Martha as the Duchess of Mougier when he introduced her to me. I realised that, against my will, I had come to observe her in close proximity, just as one approaches a tiger in its cage.

It was on me that Martha – 'Duchess of Mougier', Flora's maid, Gildas's mistress – conferred the honour of the next dance. She placed her gloved hands on my upper arms with a grace and eagerness that distressed me as much as it did her other suitors. I saw Henry de Choiseux make as if to intervene, ready for anything; but, no doubt remembering that he had already exacted my life in the duel that was to take place the following day, he must have decided that he could do no more. The three men who barred Martha's way onto the dance floor melted away to let us pass, but there was something solemn, thwarted, furious and frustrated in the way they stepped aside that attracted attention.

I danced with Martha, at first without a word, bewildered and stunned but still conscious, despite myself, of the closeness of her body that seemed made of iron and silk and flesh more carnal than that of other women.

'Well,' she said lightly, with barely any inflection. 'Well?'

'You were all that was missing,' I replied, and she burst out laughing.

Her laughter was the gayest, the most childlike, the most innocent and infectious I had ever heard in my life. It was laughter that contained all laughter, just as her cry a while before seemed the very essence of love; and it was laughter to which I finally succumbed and which drove us, in a great state of hilarity concealed behind our masks, into the adjoining room, where we fell onto a bergère. To this day, I do not know what possessed me, whether I was laughing at life, at us, whether it was the laughter of despair or of a giggling schoolboy, whether it was wicked or nervous; or whether the tone in which I had uttered those unhappy words – 'You were all that was missing' – had really been funny.

It was almost two o'clock, when we would all have to remove our masks, a prospect I little relished considering how bruised and horribly swollen my face. must be with tears of sadness and merriment; and nor indeed did Martha, who would of course have to leave before then. I imagined for a moment the expression on Choiseux's face if he realised he had been paying court to a chambermaid, and I was seized anew with laughter. I explained to Martha what had prompted my irrepressible hilarity and she was highly amused. Flora passed by, and smiled when she saw us. Gildas, whose arm she was holding, turned towards us the face of a condemned man, a face that was livid, arrogant, suspicious, betrayed, deceived, deceitful, exhausted. And my fit of laughter was quite stemmed by the memory of what awaited me at dawn. Martha wanted to know the reason for my sudden low spirits and I realised that, having only just joined the festivities and not knowing any of the guests – with good cause – our fraudulent duchess knew nothing of what had happened.

'To cut a long story short, I am going to get myself killed,' I mumbled as I finished telling her my tale of woe. 'I can handle a pencil, a horse or a pen, but under no circumstances can I usefully avail myself of a sword. As for a pistol, I believe I once killed a thrush when I was aiming at a boar . . .'

I felt strangely at ease in the company of this demonically inspired lady's maid. Her audacity in appearing at this ball, in calling herself a duchess, in abusing the rich and the powerful from round about, suddenly struck me as more a matter of daring than effrontery. I confess I felt a sort of confused admiration for this whore who shared her favours between two footmen, a prefect, some tramps, and a peasant-poet. My eyes must have betrayed my thoughts, because behind her mask her grey eyes seemed to become more limpid as she responded to words I had not uttered.

'I like you too, Lomont, I have always liked big men – strong and stupid, sentimental and clumsy – lawyers who work for the rich are generally friends of the poor. You seem a little less wicked than the others, or at least a little less conceited. Perhaps being a commoner suits you.'

'It suits me, but I shall be killed like a blue-blooded prince just the same,' I said bad-temperedly.

'Who are you drawn against? Norbert? He must be good with weapons. He's impotent. People like that are very cruel. If they can't perform as men, they want to excel at something else. That pig will most certainly have made weapons his forte.'

'Impotent?' I could not help asking, and was immediately ashamed of my curiosity.

I stood up, suddenly aware that talking to her, conversing with her, and laughing with her was to be a party to her lying; and what to her was a game would, as far as Flora was concerned, be a tragedy. She smiled when she saw me to be on the point of leaving her, and she said, 'Norbert will die before you,' as if she were promising me a piece of cake as a special treat after Sunday mass.

I returned to the ballroom, and saw that the dramatic incident which had taken place earlier, far from casting gloom on the proceedings, had on the whole revived the guests' spirits. D'Orty was certainly a marvellous host. He had some heady wines to offer, delicious food, good music, beautiful women and to cap it all a topic of conversation that outshone the most spectacular firework display. Because people were talking about the duel, it seemed. Some of the men favoured Choiseux, others Gildas – and the ladies unanimously concurred with Gildas's supporters. As for myself, I was delighted to see that I was already lamented as lost. All my clients clasped my hands in silence, their eyes moist, murmuring a few indistinct words about my talents as a man of law, and apart from one or two cynics and the odd miser who had the impertinence to ask me if I had carried out their orders as regards their investments, I was enchanted by the realisation that if they had to manage without me, it would not be without some degree of inconvenience. The Marquis of Doillac openly expressed his anxiety about a field he had been wanting me to buy on his behalf. I replied rather shortly that nothing had been done, but that I hoped to proceed with the purchase the day after tomorrow. This prompted him to shake his head pessimistically, and led me to add that if he expected me to leap on a horse to go and buy his field now, he was very much mistaken: I was not going to stay up all night before a duel for the sake of a few blades of grass. If the truth were told, it was on that day that I lost him as a client.

D'Orty on the other hand behaved with all due respect. He seemed worried by what he knew of my skills as a swordsman and a marksman. He went off to talk to the elder of the Choiseux brothers and returned despondent. The young man, who was an excellent shot, had chosen pistols and was obviously stupid enough to want to rob a man of his life who was incapable of taking his. A little earlier Gildas had suggested that he should fight both brothers, one after the other, if he survived long enough, but both brothers refused to countenance his proposal. They wanted to see my innocent blood run – since it was not blue, there was no harm in spilling it. If d'Orty was very upset, I was no less so, and more upset than terrified. To tell the truth, the idea that I might die, stupidly killed by a man whom only the day before was virtually unknown to me, and for the sake of an adorable woman but one on whom I had not even laid a finger, seemed so absurd to me that I felt only a vague sense of distaste, a sort of exasperated lassitude which was interpreted by those present as a heroic stance. I heard people praising my rashness and folly with a great deal more conviction than I had ever, during the past ten years, heard them laud my prudence or my legal judgement. Artemise went so far as to swoon in my arms and to weep openly on my shirt-front over our brief affair – one which she, however, had never wanted to consummate.

A few other ladies from the Charente who had been more responsive to my advances, as much seduced by my discretion after our lovemaking as by the degree of my passion when we embraced, took me to one side and assured me of their feelings of tenderness towards me, of the special place I should occupy in their hearts and minds the following day. It was a ghost which left that room and strolled once more along the now ghostly-seeming stairways and corridors. Gildas and Flora were waiting for me, I knew, but all at once I felt I could not bring myself to face them. I went straight to bed, and lay down determined as I have rarely been to sleep, and almost immediately I slipped into the arms of Unconsciousness, that easiest of mistresses. The last image to pass before my eyes was that of Martha waltzing, continuing to sow rivalry among her admirers.

I AWOKE DRESSED IN A white half-open shirt, in front of a pistol aimed at my heart by Norbert de Choiseux from the other end of a field. Waking up has always been a long and difficult process for me, and I have always crawled sluggishly between my bedroom and my dressing-room for about an hour before descending to my study and becoming a human being capable of thought. It was the same that morning, and despite the melodramatic aspect to that fresh white dawn, I stood shivering bad-temperedly, not knowing why I was there. I felt alone, I had no friends. Then, as I have said, I regained consciousness all of a sudden, at the last minute. I opened my eyes and saw the field, the pale blue sky, the grass levelled by the wind, the undulating landscape, the earth – my earth – the sky – my sky – and this hand – my hand – holding a heavy object that was cold and alien: a loaded pistol the very weight and feel of which horrified me. We were to duel first. I could see Gildas a little distance away, staring at the ground, and also dressed in a white shirt. And I imagined I could see, as I had done only a short time ago, Flora's haggard face swollen with tears at an open doorway.

But this dog is going to kill me, I suddenly realised. And I felt all my muscles harden more in fury than in fear.

'Gentlemen, are you ready?' said the voice of someone I did not know, who was strutting about in a top hat, well wrapped up, and safely positioned a few steps away from us. Not without good reason, for as I have said, while aiming at Choiseux I could very easily put a bullet through the head of any man present. I glanced at the man who was so anxious to see me dead, then looked away, and saw behind the hedge which marked the boundary of the field something red, a red cloth, which appeared in the bushes to the right of where Norbert was standing. I thought it must be a young farmhand lured by the prospect of seeing his loutish masters kill one another, but my opponent raised something in his right hand which caught the first rays of sunlight – as if the sun had been waiting until that pistol and no other was aimed at its prey before coming out from behind the clouds and breaking through the dawn.

'On the count of three, you may fire, gentlemen. One . . .'

And Norbert de Choiseux, assuming a firm stance, his large well-built body suddenly graceful with tension and the violent desire to kill me, fixed his eyes on me, his arm stretched out in front of him. And almost so as not to look a fool standing there with my arm hanging by my side, I too raised mine and pointed it in his general direction.

'Two,' said the voice.

Realising that my finger was not on the trigger but on the guard, I quickly moved it, and when I felt the trigger so close to my index finger, I could not prevent myself from reeling in horror. I was in that instant aware that I could never, whatever the circumstances, deliberately kill a man. It was then that I heard a strange noise, like a cat mewing or a kind of whistling, that came from somewhere on my left – that is, the opposite side to where the others were standing. It emanated from the red shawl, and was audible only to Norbert and myself. A voice cried, 'Norbert . . . Norbert . . .' and it sounded like an echo of a cry already heard. It affected me less than it did Choiseux; relaxing all the muscles in his body and, it seemed, forgetting me, he turned his head towards the noise with the quickness of a bird. I saw a smile of ecstasy, of surprise and happiness appear on his brutish face before the voice said 'Three', and I fired with my eyes shut, for the sake of doing something, however futile, before dying. When I opened my eyes again, my blood throbbing at my temples, feeling strangely and uncontrollably nauseous, I saw Norbert de Choiseux stretched out on the ground, and when I stepped closer I saw that he had been hit between the eyes, just the way that it is supposed to happen in a proper duel. There was no sign of anything red behind the hedge, but another red stain was already seeping into the grass.

Everyone looked at me in amazement and even admiration, which made me feel even more nauseous, and forced me to disgorge under a tree the breakfast I had eaten only an hour before while virtually still asleep. Martha had kept her promise.

The Choiseux were an old aristocratic family, barbaric in their customs, but closely knit. And Henry, the eldest, who had happily encouraged his younger brother in a criminal act, was devastated at having brought about his death. He threw himself on the body and called out his brother's name, sobbing in such a heart-rending manner that it brought tears to my eyes, and I would even have attempted to console him if someone had not impressed upon me with a disapproving glance how inappropriate this would be.

Gildas was pale. He looked at me in surprise, uneasy and confused. The poor boy had no doubt been preparing himself to avenge my death rather than to hear the laments of my victims. Choiseux finally calmed down, drew his pistol and, without even looking at Gildas, shot him in the arm. At the same time he was hit in the leg; he spun round and fell to the ground, where I saw him – a pathetic sight – crawl towards his brother's body, which he had refused to allow anyone to move, calling his name all the while, as if his duel with Gildas had been a meaningless interruption of his mourning. I was trembling, we were all trembling. It was all so pitiable – this pale green meadow, those two men in white shirts, covered in each other's blood, those two brothers, one bewailing the loss of the other to whom he clung, sobbing bitterly, repeating his name over and over, and paying no attention to his own shattered leg from which the bone protruded. What a miserable waste of a human life, killed by a lead bullet, and what folly those notions of birth and honour and false pride! Even the seconds seemed to feel this because the one who had given the signal to fire threw his hat to the ground and said in horror that it was the last time he would have anything to do with 'a farce of this sort', as he described it, before departing, absurd and ridiculous in his frock coat, beneath a suddenly golden sky.

For it was eight o'clock. This grotesque barbarism had taken exactly one and a quarter hours of our time. It was certainly the first time in my life that I was proud not to be a nobleman, and therefore not obliged to abide by their senseless and bloody laws.

A short while later I was with Flora and Gildas in their rooms. Flora was busy looking after her wounded lover, her eyes red with lack of sleep, torn between relief and the horror of the previous night, between her anxiety for Gildas and her joy that it was only his arm that was hit and not his head. She embraced me fervently, betraying none of the surprise that the other guests and inhabitants of the château displayed, who all looked at me as if I were a ghostly apparition, having already given me up for dead the day before. And taking me aside, Flora said with a nervous laugh, 'My goodness! What a relief that you are both still alive . . . Last night was horrible. Where did you go when we went back to the ballroom? That child . . .' she said, pointing to Gildas stretched out on his sickbed, 'that child wanted to go and dance, can you imagine, before the duel . . .' She was laughing as a mother laughs at the antics of her offspring. 'I assure you it is true. Isn't it, Gildas?' she said to her lover, who closed his eyes without turning his head. 'He even danced with that beautiful stranger, the Duchess of Mougier, whom I have never heard of before.'

'No doubt she was one of d'Orty's whores dressed up for the ball,' said Doillac, who had wandered in by chance, or had come to talk to me about his field again. 'It would not be out of character where our host is concerned.'

'Surely not,' said Flora, with that instinctive generosity of spirit that she extended even when she might have cause for jealousy. 'Surely not. There was nothing common about that woman, even if she was a little unwise in behaving as she did in the company of men. I would certainly be curious to see her again.'

'She left before dawn, Madame,' said a dull emotionless voice.

And then I noticed Martha helping the doctor to

dress Gildas's wound. She wore her usual black dress, and her hair was drawn severely back in a bun. I stared at her with amazement, gratitude, terror, and I know not what else, but she did not look up.

'Your mysterious lady left when others were coming home,' Flora laughed, looking affectionately at Martha. 'The ball in the village must have been very lively to keep you out so late,' she said without reproach. 'But anyway,' she said to Martha, 'there would not have been anything for you to do. I have been wearing this dress all night, and all this morning, and I shall hate it for the rest of my life,' she added, looking down at the blue tulle dress that she had so much liked the day before.

And as Martha still said nothing, Flora turned to me and with a fond glance in her maid's direction, remarked, 'I must say, red suits her extraordinarily well. Yesterday, I lent her my big Indian shawl – that must have sealed her success with the village beaux.'

Then she fell silent because d'Orty came in looking serious, without seeming at all comforted by the sight of his notary and his friend Gildas still alive.

'There is going to be an inquest,' he said. 'Someone has been killed. We shall have to settle on an explanation and stick to it. You do realise, do you not, that duelling is as much a crime when committed by gentlemen as by anyone else. And Choiseux has an uncle in the Upper Chamber.'

'But Honoré can give an account of what happened,' I protested. 'Honoré's the prefect, damn it. His word will not be questioned. And Choiseux is not in a position to complain about a duel which he provoked and even insisted on.'

'Choiseux is not complaining about anything,' said d'Orty, 'apart from the death of his brother. And as far as that is concerned, Lomont, he charged me to tell

184

you that he saw you close your eyes before firing, and that he holds nothing against you. His brother's bullet was found in a tree-trunk. He must have fired as he fell. And you did not shoot before the word was given. No, Choiseux will not say anything, or he will say whatever we want him to say. But Honoré will not be saying anything either. Our prefect hanged himself this morning in the barn. His body has just been found.'

There was a moment's silence so profound and so interminable that I was relieved when Flora cried out and stumbled, before falling to the ground in a faint. While Gildas tried to rise, and while d'Orty explained to the crowd of people who were gradually filling the room how Honoré's body had been found, while everyone told each other how they had seen Honoré late the previous night, and while someone was saying that they had even seen him dancing the last waltz with that mysterious and seductive stranger, I stepped out of the room, having signalled to Martha that she was to join me. She came close to me, and gazed at me with the deceptive air of an exemplary and irreproachably deferential maid, but her grey eyes were laughing like a demon's in the darkness of the corridor.

'Well then,' she said in a low voice, 'happy to be alive, my learned friend?'

'Yes,' I was forced to admit. 'Thank you. But tell me – one question, just one: Norbert de Choiseux. I saw him die. He was smiling. He was happy. He died happy. Did you not tell me he was impotent?'

I was ashamed to ask such a question at a time like this, ashamed not to be thinking of Artemise and Honoré, of the living and the dead, but this question had been drumming in my head since dawn.

'Well,' I said, 'was he impotent, or was he not?'

Martha looked at me intently, and a sort of willingness to please lit up her face when she replied with a smile: 'Yes, he was impotent from childhood.'

'Well? Well, why did he look at you, then?'

'Why? Because with me he was no longer impotent,' she said with no more pride than regret.

For a thousand reasons which I shall not go into – because suddenly I feel overwhelmed by old age and sadness, and remorse too for having taken pleasure in this melancholy tale – but for a thousand reasons the marriage between Flora and Gildas was quickly decided upon. Honoré was buried. Artemise was too readily and too quickly consoled. Then there was the marriage in the chapel in Boutteville, Flora being a Protestant by her previous marriage, and Gildas, like all peasants, an atheist or nothing at all. I was their witness. It came to the words which are used at such ceremonies, words which the priest delivered in a firm voice that still rings in my ears:

'If anyone knows cause or just impediment why this man and this woman should not be joined together . . .'

I cannot remember the exact words, but I remember seeing Martha step forward from the last row of the congregation and hearing her say: 'I do,' in a voice which froze my blood, made Gildas turn white, and stunned everyone present. I remember the terrifying silence, as she walked towards the priest until she reached Flora and Gildas, on whom she placed a sun-tanned hand, hardly spoiled by her domestic work, and she rested against him for a moment before saying in a clear voice audible for miles around, 'I married this man one month ago in Bordeaux. But I leave him to my mistress, for I am a good servant. Anyway I far prefer Mr Doillac's footman, who is waiting for me outside.'

In a silence even more profound, because Gildas had just covered his face in his hands and Flora's mouth hung open in stupefied despair, Martha added: 'You may keep my wages too, Countess,' before walking away like a queen. The effect was stunning, for the way she walked, her poise and her beauty suddenly made this outrageous declaration seem plausible.

As for the rest, what does it matter whether one knows what happened or not? What does it matter that I am the only one who remembers? I am eager to finish, too eager, but I cannot bear to recall certain memories, certain hours I spent then, that terrifying stormy autumn of despair, when the wind and the earth were at one with man's folly. So I shall be very brief in concluding this story.

The following day Gildas killed himself and Flora went mad shortly afterwards. Because of her wealth and position she was not put into an asylum but entrusted to the care of an order of nuns in Bordeaux, where she died two years later. The first time I was able to visit her, she did not recognise me, and I too barely recognised her.

Destiny was to bring me face to face with Martha once more.

After spending two years in the convent, Flora died insane, wildly insane, leaving everything to Gildas, whom she believed to be alive. Gildas, who had committed suicide, had left everything to Martha, his wife, and so too did Honoré d'Aubec, and d'Orty, who died of pleurisy not long after. I was therefore obliged to track down this fabulously wealthy heiress. I pursued her and found everywhere among the rich and eminent in our country the smouldering ruins she left in her wake. She was an unusual heiress, because wherever she went she inherited everything and left it all to the poor. She brought disaster everywhere and took nothing herself.

After four years' searching, I finally caught up with her in Paris, where she had arrived the day before the Seasons conspiracy took place. I came upon her on the barricades in the Faubourg Sainte-Antoine, killed by a bullet through the heart, smiling with an air of great gentleness which I did not recognise in her. She had died for the Revolution that we all feared, the Revolution she herself embodied perhaps . . .

STAR BOOKS BESTSELLERS

FICTION

THE PROTOCOL	*Sarah Allan Borisch*	£2.25*
GARLAND OF WAR	*Tessa Barclay*	£1.95
A SOWER WENT FORTH	*Tessa Barclay*	£2.25
SEASON OF CHANGE	*Lois Battle*	£2.25*
WAR BRIDES	*Lois Battle*	£2.50*
LET'S KEEP IN TOUCH	*Elaine Bissell*	£2.50*
FAREWELL TO BLACKOAKS	*Ashley Carter*	£1.95*
DREAMS OF GLORY	*Thomas Fleming*	£2.50*
PROMISES TO KEEP	*Thomas Fleming*	£2.25*
THE OFFICER'S WIVES	*Thomas Fleming*	£3.25*
DAYS OF ETERNITY	*Gordon Glasco*	£2.50*
THE CARDINAL SINS	*Andrew M. Greeley*	£1.95*
THY BROTHER'S WIFE	*Andrew M. Greeley*	£1.95*
ASCENT INTO HELL	*Andrew M. Greeley*	£1.95*
SISTER	*Irene Heywood Jones*	£1.80

STAR Books are obtainable from many booksellers and newsagents. If you have any difficulty tick the titles you want and fill in the form below.

Name _____

Address _____

_____

Send to: Star Books Cash Sales, P.O. Box 11, Falmouth, Cornwall, TR10 9EN.

Please send a cheque or postal order to the value of the cover price plus:
UK: 55p for the first book, 22p for the second book and 14p for each additional book ordered to the maximum charge of £1.75.

BFPO and EIRE: 55p for the first book, 22p for the second book, 14p per copy for the next 7 books, thereafter 8p per book.

OVERSEAS: £1.00 for the first book and 25p per copy for each additional book.

While every effort is made to keep prices low, it is sometimes necessary to increase prices at short notice. Star Books reserve the right to show new retail prices on covers which may differ from those advertised in the text or elsewhere.

*NOT FOR SALE IN CANADA

STAR BOOKS ADULT READS

FICTION

DARKNESS COMES	*Dean R. Koontz*	£2.25*
WHISPERS	*Dean R. Koontz*	£2.25*
NIGHT CHILLS	*Dean R. Koontz*	£2.50*
SHATTERED	*Dean R. Koontz*	£1.80*
PHANTOMS	*Dean R. Koontz*	£2.25*
CHASE	*Dean R. Koontz*	£1.95*
ALL OR NOTHING	*Stephen Longstreet*	£2.50*
BODIES AND SOULS	*John Rechy*	£2.50*
THE PAINTED LADY	*Francoise Sagan*	£2.25*
THE STILL STORM	*Francoise Sagan*	£1.95*
THE BODY	*Richard Ben Sapir*	£2.50*
THUNDERHEADS	*Colin Sharp*	£2.25
LAMIA	*Tristan Travis*	£2.75*
SCORCHED EARTH	*Edward Fenton*	£1.95
AGAINST ALL GODS	*Ashley Carter*	£1.95*
BREAST STROKE	*Molly Parkin*	£1.95

STAR Books are obtainable from many booksellers and newsagents. If you have any difficulty tick the titles you want and fill in the form below.

Name _____

Address _____

_____

Send to: Star Books Cash Sales, P.O. Box 11, Falmouth, Cornwall, TR10 9EN.

Please send a cheque or postal order to the value of the cover price plus:
UK: 55p for the first book, 22p for the second book and 14p for each additional book ordered to the maximum charge of £1.75.

BFPO and EIRE: 55p for the first book, 22p for the second book, 14p per copy for the next 7 books, thereafter 8p per book.

OVERSEAS: £1.00 for the first book and 25p per copy for each additional book.

While every effort is made to keep prices low, it is sometimes necessary to increase prices at short notice. Star Books reserve the right to show new retail prices on covers which may differ from those advertised in the text or elsewhere.

*NOT FOR SALE IN CANADA